TAGGART

TAGGART
MURDER IN SEASON
by

Peter Cave

MAINSTREAM
PUBLISHING
in conjunction with
Scottish Television

This book is published by
SCOTTISH TELEVISION
Cowcaddens
Glasgow G2 3PR

in conjunction with
MAINSTREAM PUBLISHING COMPANY
(EDINBURGH) LTD.
7 Albany Street
Edinburgh EH1 3UG

ISBN 0 906391 94 6 (H/B)
ISBN 0 906391 95 4 (P/B)

From the series written by Glenn Chandler

Executive Producer   Robert Love
Producer   Haldane Duncan
Director   Peter Barber-Fleming

Typeset by Studioscope in conjunction with
Mainstream Publishing.
Printed by The Guernsey Press Company Limited, Guernsey, C.I.

Chapter One

FROM the library window, Mulholland had only seen the nose of the Range Rover turning into the drive. As he opened the front door, the trailer, and the gleaming new cabin cruiser it transported, came as a surprise to him.

"Expecting the flood, John?"

John Samson looked up from unhitching the trailer at the sound of his father-in-law's voice. He grinned proudly. "What do you think of her?"

"Beautiful. As beautiful as ever."

Samson frowned slightly, following Mulholland's gaze towards the front passenger seat of the Range Rover before he understood. He flashed the older man a faintly chiding, faintly challenging look — the look peculiar to two men when an attractive woman is the subject.

"I meant the boat." The words were superfluous, but said anyway.

Kirsty King started to climb out of the Range Rover. Mulholland moved quickly to meet her, smiling warmly. He was glad John had brought her. A touch of glamour still stirred his ailing, seventy-year-old heart with a minimum of danger. The urge remained, even when the opportunities had long since declined.

Mulholland embraced Kirsty with genuine affection and a hint of the half-expected lechery. He kissed her briefly on the cheek, appreciating the faint and discreet aroma of Chanel.

"Hello, Mr Mulholland." Kirsty smiled up at him, enduring the sustained contact.

It was a good enough excuse for another squeeze.

"I've told you a dozen times . . . it's Frank."

"Mind if I leave her in the drive over the weekend?" Samson had finished unhitching the trailer and was screwing on the brake.

"Aye. Of course. Perhaps you'd like to leave Kirsty with me too?"

"No chance." The reply was half-joking, half-serious. The serious half was as clear an indication of male possession as a dog

5

scenting a tree or a patch of grass.

Mulholland discreetly disentangled himself from the girl, turning his attention to the cruiser. "She's certainly a lovely craft. Must have set you back a few thousand. The company must be doing well since I turned it over to you."

"The company's doing fine, Frank. And none the poorer for this bit of business, I assure you."

"Ah!" Mulholland nodded understandingly, and without a trace of rebuke. So the boat was a kick-back, a sweetener. He had not built a multi-million pound business up from scratch without accepting the inevitable degree of persuasion. Mulholland would have baulked at the word corruption, even though one was a euphemism for the other.

"Anyway — go aboard, have a look around if you want to. Kirsty and I have to get going. I promised Graeme we'd go and watch his rugby match."

Samson ushered Kirsty back into the Range Rover and skirted around the front. On an afterthought, he turned back to his father-in-law. "Would you not like to come yourself?"

Mulholland shook his head. "I would, John, but Doctor MacNaughton said he was popping in some time this morning. I'd best wait for him."

"Nothing wrong, Frank?"

"Of course not. He just likes to frighten me from time to time. And sample my Islay malt."

Samson nodded, opened the door and slid into the Range Rover. He backed it away from the cruiser in a sweeping half-circle, a trifle hard on the accelerator and quick on the clutch. The Range Rover disappeared off down the drive, leaving a huge question mark carved into the gravel.

Mulholland watched them go, ignoring the minor damage. He was still thinking of Kirsty, feeling her, smelling her. Trying to remember the last time he held a 23-year-old with the face and figure of a *Playboy* centrefold in his arms. Too long, anyway. But then he'd had a fair run, in his day. With a wistful grin creasing his rugged old features, Mulholland started to climb up into the cabin cruiser to inspect the latest company acquisition.

Kirsty gave an exaggerated shiver as they drove out through the big iron gates. "Ugh! I thought the old bugger was never going to let go of me."

Samson smiled goodnaturedly, not taking his eyes off the road. "Oh, Frank's all right."

Kirsty was not convinced. "Well he gives me the creeps. There's something . . . weird about the whole set-up. Him . . . you . . . me . . . everything."

"Weird?" This time Samson half-turned to look at her.

"It just doesn't seem natural, any of it. You walk out on his daughter after twelve years of marriage — and what does he do? Hands over the family business to you. He treats you like his oldest and dearest friend, you go shooting together every chance you can . . . and when you start bringing home a girlfriend, he not only accepts me without a murmur, he does his damnedest to get in a quick grope himself. Yes, weird is a fairly accurate word, I would say."

Samson sensed that she was genuinely upset. He explained gently. "Look, Kirsty — Frank handed the business over to me simply because I was the only man for the job. Not just because I knew the business inside out, but because of my connections on the local council. It was sound business sense, that's all. As far as our friendship is concerned — I like him. He doesn't blame me for the breakdown of our marriage so there's no grudge to bear. He and Eleanor were never really close as father and daughter, anyway. There was always a guarded distance, a coolness — as though they shared some slightly unpleasant secret which was never brought out into the open."

Samson broke off as they drove into view of the school rugby ground. The match was in full swing.

"Listen . . . talking of coolness, love . . . could you please try to be a bit more friendly towards Graeme? I know it must be difficult facing a prospective stepson who's only five years younger than you are — but it makes things awkward for me too, you know. You seemed to get on so well when you first met. It's just the last few times . . ."

"I'll shower him with maternal love, John." Kirsty was unusually snappy. Wisely, Samson let the matter drop right there.

Detective Inspector Jim Taggart's face bore an expression of aggrieved boredom. The soaring, swooping liquid notes of an accomplished mezzo soprano failed to stir anything in him except a sense of ordeal.

Taggart didn't like opera. He didn't like operetta, classical music or string quartets. By the same token, he didn't like pop music either, and loathed — to quote his own words — the painted-up pansies who performed it.

There wasn't much, musically, that Taggart *did* like. There was a time when he had been a particularly fervent fan of the Rolling Stones — but then that was two decades ago. Middle age had soured Taggart's mind as completely as his body.

He shifted irritably in the hard wooden seat, searching the bare walls of the improvised concert hall for some distraction. There was none. Taggart glanced sideways to catch a glimpse of Jean's enraptured expression, and felt a renewed sense of sadness and detachment.

He was out of place, and it wasn't just the music. It was physical. One man, basically sound of mind and limb surrounded by a sea of wheelchairs.

Taggart sighed under his breath. God, how he *hated* these affairs for the Disabled Foundation. Attending them, trying to share his wife's world, was supposed to bring them closer together, sustain the deep love they had once known. Instead, Taggart was merely reminded of the gulf between them, a black hole of communication which grew larger by the day.

It had been so different in the early days, after Jean's paralysis following the birth of their only daughter. Then, there had been a strange, savage and powerful beauty in his pity, his terrible anguish and his total love. Those first few years, when she had needed him so much and so desperately, Taggart had exulted in the consuming force of a *raison d'etre* such as few men have the privilege to know.

Now, Jean was virtually self-sufficient. She had challenged her disability with every fibre of her being, and conquered it. From then on, her path had been one of pure aggression. Charity work, sociology degrees, organising, petitioning, tilting at windmills from a two-wheeled Rozenante. She had built a new existence for herself, in which Taggart was little more than an observer. He still loved her of course, but with a sense of resigned detachment.

Taggart felt a sudden, sharp dig in the ribs, which shook him from his reverie. He was suddenly aware that the singing had stopped, and that people all around him were clapping.

Automatically, Taggart raised his arms and began slapping his open palms together, too loudly and too enthusiastically.

The applause died away. Taggart scraped his chair back against the bare wooden floor, starting to rise. Jean's gentle grip on his arm restrained him. Looking up, following her almost imperceptible nod, Taggart saw the singer bearing down on them. He shrivelled inside. God! It wasn't over yet!

She was standing over them now, her hand extended to Jean. "Mrs Taggart. I do hope the programme was what everyone wanted to hear."

Jean Taggart shook her hand warmly. "I'm sure it was. It was good of you to do it. You must be terribly busy with all your commitments."

"On the contrary. A few weeks rest before we take *The Marriage of Figaro* to Sydney. And I welcome the privilege of performing for such a worthwhile cause."

"Thank you again." Jean nodded towards Taggart. "Of course, you haven't met my husband, Jim. Jim — Eleanor Samson."

Taggart rose, stiffly, extending his hand like a challenge. It was taken up, in a warm, and surprisingly strong grip.

"Pleased to meet you. I enjoyed your performance," Taggart muttered, as enthusiastically as possible.

The faintest suggestion of a sarcastic grin cracked the professional smile. "Thank you. Nice of you to say so."

Taggart bristled inside. There it was again — in that almost imperceptible emphasis on the single word 'say'. The assumption, and the gentle reminder, that he was an outsider.

Eleanor turned back to Jean for a few more words of social chit-chat. Taggart looked at her politely, but he wasn't listening. He was firmly back in his *persona veritas*. Jim Taggart — policeman. So he assessed Eleanor Samson through his policeman's eyes.

40-ish. Blonde. Attractive. Height: 5′ 7″. Decent figure, with that tendency towards overblown chestiness that opera singers are prone to. Dominant, perhaps aggressively so. And definitely used to money long before fame. The last part was pure hunch, but Taggart trusted his hunches.

Eleanor had one last perfunctory speech before making escape.

"Nice to have met you, Mr Taggart. Perhaps we shall meet again soon."

Taggart doubted it very much. He was wrong. Eleanor Samson

was about to be thrown, suddenly and violently, into *his* world.

The rugby match was over. The players started to file off the field. Samson picked out the mud-splattered figure of his son and waved cheerily. There was no response.

Samson assumed he was sulking, his side just having narrowly lost the match. He pulled Kirsty by the hand, skirting diagonally across the field to intercept Graeme's course towards the changing rooms.

"Hey — Graeme. Hold on."

The boy stopped, looked across and nodded deferentially. "Hallo Dad." The greeting was without warmth or welcome.

Still Samson took no personal slight. He had brought the lad up to be a winner. Losing came hard. Samson ran the last few yards which separated them, rehearsing a face-saving welcome.

"Hey, that was a helluva try you made in the second half."

Graeme regarded his father sullenly. "Yes — well if you'd managed to make it for the kick-off, you'd have seen a much better one in the first."

Samson could ignore the open animosity no longer. He shrugged apologetically. "Yes, sorry. Busy . . . you know."

Graeme cast Kirsty a sneering glance. "Oh yes?" Graeme fidgeted with his feet in the mud. "Look, I've got to go. I promised to meet Mum."

The information took Samson by surprise. "I didn't know your mother was home."

Graeme sniffed. "Yes, well you wouldn't, would you?"

Samson racked his mind for something to say, some way to salvage the situation. "Look — you go and get changed and we'll give you a lift."

"No need. We've got a coach."

The boy walked off. Samson didn't try to stop him. There was no point. He turned back to Kirsty. "Come on. We might as well get back. I've got a Council Planning Meeting in a few hours."

"You're not going to leave me alone with that dirty old man of a father-in-law of yours?"

Samson smiled, unable to take her seriously. "You can get on stocking up the boat. That'll keep you out of his clutches, if you're worried about it."

Kirsty pouted sulkily. Samson sighed inwardly. He didn't seem to be able to please anyone today. And Eleanor was home. There was worse to come.

Chapter Two

GRAEME greeted his mother enthusiastically as she walked out of the concert hall. "Hi Mum."

"Graeme. What splendid timing." Eleanor threw her arms around the boy's shoulder, propelling him down the street. "They say singing is an art. So is getting away. If I'd had to sign one more autograph . . ."

"You sound tired."

"Exhausted. Six months touring, and five charity shows. I'm looking forward to my break."

Graeme gently disengaged himself from his mother's embrace, falling into step beside here. "So how was the tour?"

"If this is Frankfurt, it must be Friday. That sort of thing, you know?"

Graeme shook his head, grinning. "No, but I can imagine. Hey, is that yours?"

Eleanor had stopped beside a brand-new, silver Mercedes sports car. She smiled. "Well I'm certainly not about to steal it."

"Can I drive it?"

"Have you passed your test while I was away?"

"No . . . but I'll be careful."

Eleanor smiled indulgently, tossing him the keys. "You'd better be."

Graeme opened the door and slid into the driving seat. He reached across to unlock the passenger door before adjusting his seat position and slipping the ignition key into the lock. The car purred into life. Graeme revved up the powerful engine as much as he dared. He looked across at his mother excitedly. "Well . . . where are we going?"

"I'd like to see your grandfather first," Eleanor said.

Graeme's face fell. "Oh. Are you sure? Wouldn't you rather go home for a rest or something?"

Eleanor's face wrinkled into a frown. It was obvious that Graeme was upset about something. "What is it?"

Graeme opened his mouth to speak, then changed his mind. Perhaps Kirsty wouldn't be there. Perhaps she and his father had gone on somewhere after the match. He decided to defer the unpleasant news. "Oh . . . it's nothing. I was just worried because you said you were so tired."

His mother smiled. "I'll be fine. Anyway, I won't be stopping long."

Graeme nodded glumly, slipped the car into gear and pulled away. They drove the two miles to Mulholland's house in virtual silence.

Eleanor was surprised to see the cabin cruiser. "Hello, what's this? Grandpa taken up a new hobby since I've been away?"

"It's Dad's."

Graeme turned off the engine and faced his mother. The presence of the Range Rover in the drive meant that he had a duty to forewarn her. "Look, Mum. It might be better if you didn't go in there right now."

"Why? Because your father's here?" Eleanor smiled. "I want to see him too, Graeme. I know we've been separated for six years, but I still love your father. Who knows? I've got five weeks. Perhaps this time we can get together, talk seriously about being a family again."

"It's not that simple, Mum." Graeme dreaded what he knew he had to tell her, sooner or later. "He's changed. A lot of things have changed while you've been away."

Eleanor shrugged. "So . . . that can only be for the better." She seemed to be oblivious to Graeme's discomfort, driven by some surging force of optimism.

"Damn it, Mum. He's got a girlfriend." Graeme blurted it out with a sense of relief. There — it was out in the open.

There was a long silence. Graeme studied his mother's face, watching hope flicker and die, sharing her pain.

"I'm sorry," he said, finally, lamely.

"Sorry?"

"That I had to be the one to tell you."

Eleanor forced a smile. She reached across the car, squeezing his hand. "Better you than someone else." She paused for a while, completing her composure. "What's she like?"

Eleanor was quite unprepared for the look of hatred which crossed Graeme's face, or the vehemence in his voice. "She's a tart," he spat out.

Taken aback, Eleanor could only shrug. "Well, your father is old enough to make his own choices." Then, after another brief pause. "Shall we go in?"

Graeme nodded, relieved that his mother seemed to have taken it all in her stride.

They climbed out of the car and crunched across the drive to the door.

Mulholland answered it, looking awkward and embarrassed. "Hello, Eleanor."

"Hello, Dad. Well, do we get invited in or not?"

Mulholland's eyes searched her face then flicked to meet Graeme's. He phrased the question written clearly on his face. "Does she know?"

Graeme nodded. "She knows."

"You'd best come in then." Mulholland stood back, ushering them inside. He showed them into the empty drawing room. Eleanor glanced around carefully.

"Where are they, then?"

"Upstairs," Mulholland said.

Eleanor raised one delicate eybrow, her lips curling into a sneer. "Really? And it's only 12.30 in the morning."

"Getting things ready for the boat," Mulholland added, hastily.

"I brought you a present," Eleanor announced suddenly, as though she had dismissed the previous matter from her mind. She delved into her bag and brought out a bottle of Calvados. "Still your favourite?"

Mulholland nodded. "As long as you don't let Doctor MacNaughton see it." He reached across, taking the bottle. "Thanks."

As if on an afterthought, Mulholland seemed to realise that a simple thankyou wasn't enough. He stepped forward stiffly, putting one arm around Eleanor's shoulder. The embrace was without real affection, almost formal. "So — how was the tour?"

"Hectic. And how are you?"

"No so hectic. A quiet life, that's the prescription these days, according to MacNaughton."

"And the company?"

"Fine. John's doing very well. Making more money than I ever did." Mulholland broke off, as they heard voices on the stairs. He shot Eleanor an awkward, pleading look. "Here they come. Look

. . . Eleanor . . .."

"Don't worry. There won't be a scene," Eleanor assured him. She turned to face the drawing-room door, bracing herself for the confrontation.

Kirsty was giggling about something as they entered the room. It died on her lips as she saw Eleanor. Her face froze into a defiant stare.

Samson just looked surprised, Mulholland embarrassed. Eleanor's drama training swung into an Oscar-winning performance. She smiled sweetly, even though Kirsty's appearance had shocked her. She had not expected the girl to be so young, or so strikingly beautiful.

"Hello, John," Eleanor purred. "Graeme told me you had a little friend for company these days."

Samson drew in a deep breath. He glowered. "Eleanor — don't start. Not here, not now."

It was Graeme who broke the tension. "Well, I'm off. Just remembered I promised to meet someone." Without another word, he dived for the door, pushing roughly past Kirsty into the hallway. The front door opened and slammed.

In the drawing room, an icy silence had descended.

"I'd like to talk, John," Eleanor said, finally, in a calm, quiet voice.

Samson nodded resignedly. "Yes." He slid his arm gently around Kirsty's waist. "Look, love . . . why don't you go out and finish sorting things out on the boat?"

The girl shrugged. "Yes, all right. If that's what you want." She threw one last, hopefully withering look at Eleanor and made her exit.

Mulholland coughed awkwardly, trying to think of a plausible excuse to leave them alone. He seized on the first thing which came to mind. "Oh . . . I said I'd take a look at that Purdey of yours. Trigger mechanism, wasn't it?"

Samson nodded absently. "Feels a bit stiff on the second barrel."

"I'll give it an overhaul and a general clean," said Mulholland. "Can't start off the new season with a faulty gun. I'll be in my workshop."

Mulholland left, closing the door behind him. Samson leaned back against the wall, regarding Eleanor. "So — you want to talk.

Anything in particular, or just general social topics?"

"I don't want to waste my voice, John. I need it."

Samson let out a short, bitter laugh. "Oh yes, your precious voice. The number of times I backed down in arguments to save that. That was when you could even stay around long enough to *have* an argument, of course."

"I had my career."

"Exactly. You had a choice between your career and our marriage. You made that choice, Eleanor. Six years ago."

"I'm home for five weeks. Time to discuss our future, put the past behind us once and for all."

Samson shook his head. "No. It's too late. There *is* no future for you and I. Not together, anyway." He paused, taking a breath. "I want a divorce, Eleanor."

"What? So you can marry her? Your Page Three girl?"

"So I can be free to . . . if I want."

Eleanor laughed sarcastically. "My God, John . . . you're ridiculous. Have you thought what a handicap she would be to you? A councillor with a wife young enough to be his daughter? Where did you meet her, anyway? A strip club?"

Samson refused to be needled. "She was working for Maxwell, the builder. In the office. Now she's with me. Has been for three months."

"Have you thought of Graeme's feelings?"

"Did you?" Samson countered. "He was ten years old when you chose your career. At least I was in one place while he grew up. He's old enough to make his own life now . . . and that's exactly what *I* want to do."

"What — spend the next few years of your life buying expensive presents to impress her? Until she gets tired of you and finds a younger man? Is that the reason for the boat?"

"We're going on holiday tomorrow. Sailing for two weeks," Samson said flatly.

Eleanor was momentarily crushed. Her face fell. Samson pressed his advantage. "Is that all, Eleanor? I have a Council meeting in less than an hour."

Eleanor came back fighting. "No, John. That's not all. Far from it. You may want to make a fool of yourself, but I'm not going to let you."

Samson sighed. "You can't stop me, Eleanor."

Tears were pricking out in Eleanor's eyes. Her voice was choked and jumpy, half emotion and half bluster. "You just damn well wait and see," she threatened. With that, she spun on her heel and stormed out of the room. Seconds later, Samson heard the slamming of the front door and Eleanor's footsteps on the gravel drive. Then the sound of the Mercedes firing into life and accelerating away with a squeal of brakes.

Eleanor's temporary burst of helpless anger had dissipated even before she got to the gates at the end of the drive. As she waited to ease out into the main road, a cold and ruthless rationality washed over her. She adjusted the rear-view mirror until the cabin cruiser came into view. She caught a glimpse of Kirsty, struggling with a heavy five-gallon petrol can. Even from that distance the girl looked stunning.

Eleanor's thoughts were of survival, self-protection. So this little blonde dolly bird wanted to take her husband away from her, did she? Well, not without a fight, Eleanor vowed silently. Not while she still had a trace of the alley cat in her womanhood. Not while she could still kick and spit and scratch with the rest of them.

She eased out into the road, switching her left-hand indicator on almost immediately. There was a small lane which skirted up the back of Mulholland's garden. Eleanor drove up it slowly, until she was more or less on a level with the house. She had a clear view of the drive, and the cruiser, through the surrounding hedge. Eleanor watched . . . and waited.

Doctor MacNaughton finished his examination and slipped his stethoscope back into his bag.

"Well, are you ready to measure me up while you're at it?" Mulholland asked.

MacNaughton smiled. "You're not ready for your box yet, Frank. You're incorrigible, but not incurable. Plenty of rest, stay off the hard stuff and take up a nice relaxing sport like fishing . . . that's my prescription."

Mulholland grunted, unimpressed. "First two signs of insanity — talking to yourself and going fishing. What do you doctors know, anyway?"

"Ah, you're a terrible old man, Frank Mulholland. You don't trust doctors, that's part of your trouble."

Mulholland grinned wickedly. "I don't trust *young* doctors, that's for sure." He paused. "Though I have to admit your father used to give me the same advice. You're as much of a killjoy as he was. Hereditary Presbyterianism, no doubt."

MacNaughton shared the joke for a few seconds. Then it was time for the banter to stop. He looked at Mulholland earnestly.

"Try to think of your heart as an elderly dog, Frank. It wants plenty of rest, not pulling around all over the place."

"How long . . . seriously?"

"Ten years — or ten weeks. It really is up to you. It's as simple as that."

Mulholland nodded, falling silent.

It was not the right note on which to leave. MacNaughton broke into a smile again. "I hear Eleanor's back for a while, by the way. Be a nice bit of company for you."

Mulholland sniffed. "Oh, I won't see much of her. I'm a hotel, that's all."

MacNaughton stood, zipping up his bag. "Oh well, give her my regards, anyway. And now I must be going. Remember what I said."

"Yes, I will," Mulholland lied, following him to the door. A sudden thought struck him. "Oh — I nearly forgot. Those Deed of Covenant papers I signed . . . for that Hospice you're setting up?"

MacNaughton seemed suddenly irritable, impatient. "The Heathervale project . . . yes, what about it?"

"Just that I checked my bank statement the other day. The donation doesn't seem to have been deducted from my account. Just thought you ought to know, that's all."

"I'll look into it. Goodbye Frank." MacNaughton closed the door behind him. Outside in the hallway, he sucked his teeth in vexation, mentally berating himself. He had been sloppy, not putting those papers through the proper channels. He couldn't afford a silly slip-up like that to upset all his carefully-made plans. There was too much at stake.

Stepping outside, MacNaughton heard raised angry female voices. He looked over towards the cruiser where Eleanor and Kirsty were arguing something out, just the one wrong word short of physical violence. Neither woman noticed him. Discretion seemed to be the order of the moment, MacNaughton thought. It was not the time to exchange social graces with Eleanor. He walked to his car slowly, deep in thought. He sat watching the two women through the side window for several minutes. Eventually Kirsty seemed to tire of the argument and climbed up into the boat. Eleanor followed her, flaming with anger. They disappeared into the interior of the cabin.

MacNaughton started his car, slipped it into gear and eased away down the drive.

Chapter Three

THE bar of the Firhill Tavern was small, dark, dingy and decrepit. It was an anachronism, a time capsule from a previous age of austerity and oppression, when an exploited and underpaid working class sought only a place to drink, get drunk and drown out the grinding boredom of their lives.

There was little or no concession to the concept of social drinking, let alone enjoyment. The wooden seats and benches were as hard and bare as the floor. A battered old dartboard on one wall provided the pub's sole entertainment. A tarnished heated display cabinet containing a few shrivelled pies was the full extent of the catering facilities.

Keith Brennan hated it — as much as he hated the shrew of a wife who kept him there, scratching a living from the ever-dwindling number of regulars. Lilly had been a harridan when he married her, but there had been compensating features. Always thin and without much of a figure, her narrow face with its high cheekbones and finely-chiselled nose had given her a slightly aristocratic look which almost passed for beauty. Plus the fact that her elderly, very sick father had held the freehold on the Firhill, and Brennan had foreseen the massive re-development in that part of the Green City.

The Firhill now sat on prime building land, its site alone worth ten times its annual profits. More than enough to buy another nice little business in a more congenial part of the countryside.

Brennan had his own little dream. An old country pub down in Devonshire. Thatched roof, oak beams, horse brasses on the walls and a little beer garden outside. A regular local trade with a welcome seasonal boost from the tourists. Plenty of bar staff, a bistro-style restaurant and holidays in Tenerife or the Greek Islands. Alas, it remained a dream, for Lilly had repeatedly refused to capitalise on their asset. Disillusioned, Brennan had taken little interest in the Firhill or his wife. Over the years, both had sunk into equal states of disrepair.

Lilly's finely-chiselled features were now merely sharp — like her tongue. Years of wearing a constantly sour expression had etched deep lines which ran downwards from the corners of her mouth, giving her the appearance of a rather emaciated ventriloquist's dummy.

Brennan had considered leaving her a thousand times, and never quite managed to do it. He would have had little trouble making a new life for himself. At the age of 45, Brennan's face was still remarkably youthful, and when not subjected to Lilly's abuse, capable of creasing into a boyish grin which women found attractive. His body bore the heritage of an athletic youth, kept in trim by regular exercise.

Financially, he had a small nest-egg which Lilly knew nothing about. For years, Brennan had salted away the odd few pounds from the profits into a private bank account. Although the Firhill was no goldmine, it afforded them a basic living with low overheads, and Brennan had never indulged himself in any expensive vices. As a result, he could have laid his hands on five or six thousand pounds at any time — more than enough to finance his initial escape.

Walking out on Lilly was one thing. Walking out on the sales potential of the Firhill was quite another. One day, Brennan kept telling himself — one day he would manage to persuade Lilly to sell up. So he waited, getting on with the day-to-day running of the pub and letting Lilly's bullying wash over him as much as possible. Outside opening hours, he had his photography, which had grown from a simple hobby into a consuming passion. Lilly resented it deeply, and lost no opportunity to make this fact obvious. Coming into the bar from the small parlour at the back of the pub, she saw one now.

Brennan had his favourite Nikon camera on the counter, and was showing off his latest batch of prints to a bored and half-drunk customer. "I took this interior shot with the new 1000 ASA film. See what detail you get, even in poor light. See that beam, by the way? Over 350 years old. So hard you couldn't knock a nail into it . . ."

"Keith!" Lilly's harsh voice shrieked across the bar like Japanese bagpipes. "Stop showing off those silly snapshots and get some glasses washed."

Brennan obeyed, meekly. Time had proven it the best technique for survival. Only one hour to go, and he could be out amongst the architecture and landscapes of the city, viewing it through the peaceful detachment of a reflex lens. He moved to the small washing-up sink and began to swill pint glasses in hot water. Lilly came over to stand over him, eyes glinting.

"No wonder we're losing trade. You drive them all away with your boring camera talk. If they want to look at snapshots, I expect they all have their own wee Instamatics at home."

Normally Brennan would have remained silent, but Lilly had given him an opening too good to pass up. "Things are slack because we're sitting in the middle of a giant building site, Lilly. We should sell up — now. Three years ago we had that offer from Mulholland. It was a good offer then . . . must be worth twice that now."

Lilly stiffened. "Will you stop flapping your useless mouth, Keith Brennan. I've told you — we're no' selling the one bit of security we've got, and there's an end to it." She stalked off in a huff. Brennan glared after her, the old familiar knot of hate tightening up in his stomach. There *had* to be a way, his mind screamed. There had to be a way to get Lilly out of his life and the Firhill into his hands.

Brennan fired off three quick shots in a row, cursing under his breath as the familiar smooth purr of the automatic wind-on was marred by a grating sound. He'd forgotten to count the number of shots left. Now the film had pulled out of the spool. He'd have to go home and open the camera up in the darkroom. Just as he was getting into his stride, beginning to relax.

The little run-in with Lilly had upset him more than usual, jangled up his nerves. Things were getting worse, Brennan realised. His hobby had previously been safe, inviolate. Now Lilly's poison was beginning to spoil that as well.

The realisation brought a sudden and chilling rationality to his mind, cooling the last vestiges of his simmering anger. Brennan *knew*, with absolute certainty, that he could no longer play the waiting game. It was time for positive action. But what could he do on his own? What he needed was an ally, a partner in crime, as it were.

Brennan had thought in the past of going to see John Samson, now that he had taken over the day-to-day running of Mulholland's property development company. Perhaps Samson would make a new, and vastly improved, offer, one which even

Lilly couldn't refuse. Samson might be prepared to tackle her directly, use some sort of pressure or coercion. He might succeed where Brennan had continually failed.

It was something to be reconsidered. Brennan walked thoughtfully back towards the Firhill, running the possible ramifications over in his head. The major snag became quickly obvious. Even if Lilly could be persuaded to sell . . . even if by some miracle he could make her leave Glasgow and go South . . . the little Devonshire pub would still be a flawed dream. It would have Lilly in it. Lilly would have control of the finances, Lilly would give the orders, Lilly would insult and drive away the customers.

Lilly! A name with which to conjure demons. Lilly, Lilly. Lilly bloody Lilly!

Brennan stopped abruptly, just about to walk into the road. He looked across it and beyond, at a skyline dominated by the high-rise tower of a Sixties housing project. Tall . . . and ugly, he thought. Just like her. In a sudden, childish fantasy, Brennan swung the useless camera around his neck up to eye level. Sympathetic magic; an exorcism of the mind. The camera was a high-powered rifle, the shutter release the trigger. Brennan zoomed up the facade of the tower, framing in on the seventh-floor window which was Lilly's heart. He pumped off six shots in a cold fury, and was only mildly surprised when the block did not come tumbling to the ground.

The silly game had served its purpose. He felt calmer now, and just a little foolish. He grinned to himself. 'Brennan, you're cracking up'. He dropped the camera, letting it dangle from its lanyard. He waited momentarily as a fire engine raced by, alarm system going full blast. Then he walked across the road, heading for the womb-like security of his darkroom.

Dense, oily black smoke filled Mulholland's drive. The cabin cruiser was an inferno, roaring tongues of flame sucked from its interior by convection and the slight breeze. Most of the superstructure had already been destroyed, leaving a blackened and twisted hulk.

The blaze looked worse than it actually was, once the firemen got to work. Foam and water soon doused the flames, the black smoke was quickly replaced by steam. Visibility cleared.

"Body over here, sir." One of the fire crew called to the chief. The fire chief handed over control of the damping spray to a colleague. He ran across the edge of the drive. Mulholland's still form lay sprawled half across the gravel, half across the grass. He was face down, knees drawn up to the stomach.

The fire chief slid his fingers under Mulholland's neck, feeling for the artery at the side of the throat. There was a faint pulse. He moved forward Mulholland's head slightly, laying his cheek on the gravel and pulling the lower jaw open.

"He's still alive. Ambulance on the way?"

The young fireman nodded. "And the police."

"Good." Satisfied he had done as much as he could for Mulholland, the chief straightened up, jerking his head towards the hissing, steaming wreck of the cruiser. "There's another one inside . . . at least, what's left of the poor bastard."

Climbing from his car, Taggart felt like a man arriving at his own funeral. Late, and rather superfluous. He reviewed the personnel assembled in Mulholland's drive.

Two uniformed constables, a fire crew, four ambulance men, the new Superintendent of Police . . . and Detective Sergeant Livingstone.

Peter Livingstone was already walking over to meet him. "Glad you got here, sir."

"Safely . . . or eventually?" Taggart gave him a withering look. "And how come you're here like the first crocus of Spring? Into telepathy now, are we?"

Livingstone let the sarcasm pass. The more he got to know and understand Taggart, the more he saw behind the bluster. He had already learned to respect his superior. Livingstone felt sure that if he kept at it, he might end up liking him as well. "I was talking to McVitie, the new Super. He gave me a ride down."

Taggart raised one eyebrow a fraction of an inch. "Annual General Meeting of the Old Boys' Association was it?"

Livingstone was one of the new young breed of copper. A university graduate, with a working knowledge of forensics, ballistics and all the other fringe police activities which had previously been the exclusive domain of outside experts. Taggart found it hard not to resent the young man's bright future in the force. Good money, early promotion and a wide circle of friends from the professions. It seemed a world away from his own past, pounding a beat, struggling up through the ranks and waiting for nearly 25 years for a decent wage.

"What's the Biscuit doing here anyway?" Taggart asked.

"Biscuit?" Livingstone looked puzzled.

"McVitie. What's a newly-promoted Superintendent doing at a domestic fire scene?"

"I gather he knows the family."

Taggart glanced at the house and surrounding grounds. "Yes, I suppose he would, wouldn't he? Well, let's get down to it, young Peter."

Taggart strode across towards McVitie, with Livingstone tagging behind. "Morning sir. I've heard of burning your boats — but not on dry land."

McVitie was not amused. He scowled at Taggart. "Hardly a humorous matter, Jim. The body's in the cabin. It's not a pretty sight."

"They seldom are, sir. Anyway, we're not here for the scenery."

Taggart moved to the burned-out cruiser, touching the outside gingerly in case it was still hot. Satisfied, he pulled himself up on to the trailer and clambered into the boat.

He entered the cabin. The corpse sat propped up against the skeletal frame of a bunk. It was completely charred, with no face. The arms were pulled up into a grotesque boxing stance, fists clenched. Taggart could only assume that it had once been human. The sickly stench of burned flesh was overpowering. Taggart pulled a handkerchief from his pocket, holding it over his nose and mouth. He heard Livingstone splashing through the flooded cabin behind him.

"Pugilistic pose," Livingstone observed. "Caused by contraction of the muscles in intense heat."

Taggart didn't want to take a second look. He flicked his eyes around the cabin, lighting on a blackened five-gallon can. He bent over it, removing his handkerchief long enough to take a quick sniff at the spout. "Petrol." Taggart left the can where it was and backed away. He turned, and headed for fresh air.

Livingstone moved towards the corpse, stooping over it. He examined the head and neck closely for several seconds before backing out of the cabin, sweeping his eyes from side to side as he did so.

Outside, Taggart quizzed the two young constables. "Who raised the alarm?"

"The neighbour. That side." One of the policemen jerked a thumb.

"And the guy lying on the ground. Who is he?"

"Frank Mulholland, sir. This is his house."

"You know who Frank Mulholland is, do you Jim?"

Taggart hadn't heard McVitie walk up behind him. He felt vaguely irritated. "No, sir. I don't."

"He's the father of Eleanor Samson, the singer. You've heard of her, perhaps?"

"Heard of her? We're personally acquainted."

A faint look of chagrin crossed McVitie's face. Taggart found it hard to repress a smile of satisfaction.

"Any theories?" McVitie nodded towards the burned-out cruiser, changing the subject.

Taggart shook his head. "Can't even speculate on the sex of the victim yet. Perhaps I'll have more to go on when I have the medical report and the fire investigator's findings." He broke off as Samson's Ranger Rover pulled into the drive. "Ah — here's someone who might give us the victim's name, at least."

McVitie looked at him quizzically. "Hunches, Jim?"

"Hardly." Taggart allowed himself the smug smile he had foregone earlier. He rattled off the registration number of the Range Rover then turned to look, pointedly at the plate of the back of the boat trailer.

"That's the trouble with a desk job, sir. You get rusty."

Taggart spun on one heel, with McVitie glaring daggers into his back. The Range Rover had squealed to a halt. Taggart moved to intercept Samson as he jumped down from the vehicle.

"Detective Inspector Taggart. Maryhill Division." Taggart flashed his ID card.

Samson didn't seem to hear him. His eyes were riveted on the charred wreck. His mouth hung slackly open.

Taggart gave the man a few seconds to recover. He read the legend written on the side of the Range Rover. ZEUS PROPERTY DEVELOPMENT. His eyes flicked round the vehicle's interior before returning to Samson. "I have to ask you some questions, Mr . . . ?"

"Samson. John Samson. My God, what happened?"

"It was your boat, I take it?"

Samson nodded dumbly.

"You live here?"

"No, my father-in-law. I left the boat for the weekend." Samson seemed to snap out of a bad dream suddenly. He looked around distractedly, panic breaking out on his face. "Where is he? Where's Kirsty?" Samson looked at the wreck anew, suddenly seeing it as more than just a burned-out boat. The implications he had at first missed struck him now.

"Oh no! Is she . . ."

"There was a body in the cabin," Taggart said flatly. The years had taught him that there was no gentle way to announce death.

"Oh my God." Samson raised his hands to his face, covering his eyes. He sobbed twice, then recovered himself with an effort. He took several deep breaths. "I desperately need a drink, Inspector. Do you mind if we go into the house?"

"Of course." Taggart followed him up the drive.

The ambulance drove off to deliver the body to the mortuary. Livingstone buttonholed Andrews, the police surgeon, as he headed towards his car.

"Find anything?"

Andrews regarded the young man irritably. "I've just conducted a brief initial examination, not a full autopsy."

"Those lacerations round the neck. What were they?"

"Splits. Contracting skin."

"There was one in particular. Went at right angles to the other."

Andrews shrugged. "Probably means nothing. Unless there's a fracture."

"Oh," Livingstone looked disappointed. "How easy to establish actual cause of death?"

Andrews had had enough. "You really are the most impatient young policeman I've worked with. Most of them at least wait until I've got my gloves off. Not easy. Perhaps impossible."

The doctor climbed into his car and drove off. Livingstone stood alone in the middle of the drive, at a loose end. Finally, he walked towards the house to sit in on Samson's statement.

"So you can't think of anyone else who might have been on the boat?" Taggart was saying.

Samson shook his head slowly. "No. It had to be Kirsty. I left her on board."

"Where did you go?"

"Planning meeting. I'm on the Council. It was postponed."

"And you came straight back here?"

"Yes. Look . . . what do you think happened out there?"

Taggart made no answer. There was none he could make. "Was petrol stored in the cabin?"

Samson nodded. "Yes. A five-gallon can."

"Did Miss King smoke?"

"Yes . . . but she'd have had no reason to open the can. It was sealed tight."

"Mind if I smell your hands, Mr Samson?"

The question took Samson by surprise. Meekly, he held out both hands and allowed Taggart to sniff them. Only then did the reason for the odd request come to him. "Oh Christ! You don't think that I . . ."

Taggart cut him short. "I don't think anything at the moment. I'm investigating a sudden death, that's all."

"Look, I've had enough." Samson stood up. "I want to phone the hospital, find out about my father-in-law."

"Close to him, are you?" Livingstone put in the question just as it was framing up on Taggart's lips.

"We're good friends — and business partners," Samson said.

"And your relationship with Miss King?" Taggart managed to inject his personal disapproval into the question.

Samson glared at him defiantly. "Not what you think. I intended to marry her . . . once Eleanor and I got a divorce."

"And how did your wife feel about that?"

Samson shrugged. "We hadn't discussed it much."

Taggart would have let it go, pedantry not being one of his foibles. Livingstone, however, seized on the single word like a terrier on a rat's back. "You said you *hadn't* discussed it, Mr Samson. Hadn't . . . past tense . . . the implication being that you have discussed the matter now. When, exactly?"

"This morning. Eleanor came to the house earlier."

"Earlier?" Taggart said.

Samson consulted his watch. "Just over two hours ago."

"Shortly before the fire started, in fact?"

"Yes, I suppose so." Samson agreed readily. Again, realisation

28

dawned late. He stared blankly at Taggart. "Eleanor?"

Taggart's face was impassive. "Did your wife meet Miss King?"

Samson nodded.

"What was her reaction?"

"Cool," Samson said, then corrected himself. "No — frosty is more accurate."

"But there was no fight . . . no argument?"

Samson shook his head. "No. Eleanor's too civilised for a common slanging match. Her precious voice, you see. Some sarcasm . . . that was all."

"And she left the house before you went to the Council meeting?"

"Yes. A good thirty minutes."

"So when you left, Miss King was on the boat and your father-in-law was alone in the house?"

"No. Just as I was leaving, Doctor MacNaughton called."

"Right. Well I don't think we need detain you any longer, Mr Samson." He glanced at Livingstone. "Unless you have any more pertinent questions?"

Livingstone shook his head, turning to the door. Taggart followed him out.

Outside, in the drive, Livingstone regarded his superior quizzically. "Hell hath no fury?"

"Could be shaping that way," Taggart agreed.

Livingstone looked down to where Mulholland had been found. "I wonder how the old man fits in?"

Taggart shrugged. "He may have got off the boat before the fire started . . . he may have been trying to get on to it to save the girl. Unless he recovers, we may never know."

Taggart walked towards his car.

"Where now?" asked Livingstone.

"Doctor MacNaughton, I think," Taggart muttered. He grinned wickedly at his colleague. "You'll be wanting a lift, I suppose? Or is the Biscuit sending a taxi for you?"

Livingstone ignored it, as usual. "Drop me off at the hospital. Mulholland may have recovered enough to talk."

Taggart grunted. He hated it when Livingstone failed to rise to his bait.

Chapter Four

MACNAUGHTON seemed genuinely concerned about Mulholland's welfare.

"We don't know his condition yet. My colleague is at the hospital now," Taggart informed him. "You saw him this morning. How is his general health?"

MacNaughton frowned slightly. "Not a well man, by any means. Quite severely hypertensive, two previous cardiacs."

Taggart nodded. "How did you know he was in the hospital?"

"They phoned me. Standard practice. I'm his GP. Where was this fire, anyway? They didn't give me any details."

Taggart ignored the question. That was his job. He didn't like giving anything away. "Do you know the family well?"

"Oh, yes. This was my father's practice before me. He was Frank's doctor from way back."

"How about a young lady — Kirsty King. Do you know her?"

"Yes. She's John Samson's . . . how do you say?"

"Did you see her this morning?"

"Yes. Briefly."

"Where?"

"Outside the house, by John's new boat. She was having an argument with Eleanor."

Taggart sucked at his teeth reflectively. Pieces were beginning to fit. "When was this?"

"As I left the house."

"Time?"

MacNaughton thought about it for a few seconds. "Probably just before one o'clock."

"So you definitely saw Eleanor Samson and Kirsty King together — and this was after John Samson had left the house," Taggart recapped.

"Yes."

"Did you speak to either woman?"

MacNaughton shook his head. "It didn't seem the right time. I'm not sure that either of them saw me."

"This argument . . . was it heated?" Taggart asked.

"Fairly."

"And did you hear anything that was said?"

"I'm not in the habit of eavesdropping, Inspector. I got into my car, saw Eleanor and Kirsty go inside the cabin, and drove off."

"You're sure of that . . . both women were inside the cabin of the boat?"

"Yes."

"And where was Mr Mulholland when you left him?"

"In his workshop. Back of the house. He was cleaning a shotgun." MacNaughton seemed a little puzzled by the depth of the interrogation. "Look, you still haven't told me where this fire was . . . or what happened."

Taggart paused for a moment, thinking about it. There seemed to be no reason for witholding the facts any longer. "Miss King was found dead in the cabin of the boat. Shortly after you left. Where did you go afterwards?"

"Afterwards?" MacNaughton seemed to take exception to the word. "I hope you're not treating me as a suspect, Inspector."

Taggart's face was expressionless. "You were one of the last three people to see the girl alive."

"I went to see an elderly patient. Mrs Harris. My receptionist can give you her address if you want it. Now you really must excuse me, Inspector. This is a busy practice. I have appointments waiting."

"Just one last thing," Taggart said, getting ready to leave. "What was Eleanor Samson wearing?"

MacNaughton closed his eyes, summoning up a mental picture. "A blue trouser suit," he said, after a while.

Taggart nodded thoughtfully, recalling his own meeting with Eleanor that morning. So she hadn't gone home to change after the concert. That was good. It kept things tidy.

Livingstone sat in the hospital corridor outside Mulholland's room. He was bored. The door opened. A nurse walked out. Livingstone jumped to his feet expectantly. "How is he?"

The nurse gave him a clinical, professional smile. "No change. He's still on the respirator. You could be in for quite a wait, I'm afraid."

Livingstone forced a grin. "Part of a copper's job. Didn't you know?"

The nurse walked away, Livingstone sighed and arched his back, stretching cramped muscles. He was about to sit down again when he saw another nurse, coming down the corridor towards him. Young. Attractive. He recognised her at once. Alison, Taggart's daughter. Livingstone preened, flicking fingers through his hair.

"Hello, Peter." Alison smiled warmly. "Is Dad here?"

"No. He's let me off the leash for once. Time off for good behaviour."

Alison laughed. "How are you two getting on these days?"

Livingstone gave her a mischievous smile. "Oh, like partners. Sparring partners. He feints, I duck. It works, just about."

"What are you doing here, anyway?" Alison asked.

"Just hanging about." Livingstone jerked his head towards the door.

"Want to hang about with me for half an hour? I'm just going down to the canteen."

Livingstone accepted the offer eagerly. He trotted down the corridor behind her like a pet puppy.

McVitie tapped perfunctorily on Taggart's door, walking in anyway. Taggart sat at his desk, catching up on paperwork.

"Anything, Jim?"

"Aye," Taggart grunted, without looking up. "Preliminary report from the fire inspector. Definitely arson, no question about it. Petrol was splashed all over the cabin interior."

"So it's murder," McVitie said quietly.

Taggart looked up then, a faintly wry grimace tugging at one corner of his mouth. "Did you ever doubt it?"

"No, not really," McVitie shook his head. "Autopsy report?"

"Doc Andrews is coming in with it later this evening," Taggart told him. "One thing *is* definite — the victim's identity. It's Kirsty King all right. She'd had some very expensive dental work done."

"Next of kin?"

"Father. All in hand. I've sent a young constable to bring him in for the formal ID." Taggart broke off for a moment, his face grim. "Look, Sir . . . do we *really* have to put him through that?"

"We don't make the rules, Jim. Just follow them. Next of kin must make, or attempt to make, a formal identification of the corpse."

Taggart sighed resignedly. McVitie had said exactly what he would have said to one of his own juniors. "Aye. Poor bastard," he added. He was thinking of Alison.

The phone rang. Taggart snatched it up. It was Livingstone. Mulholland had come round, and was well enough to talk.

"I'll be there in fifteen minutes," Taggart said, putting the receiver back. He appraised McVitie of the situation. "Do you want to come?"

McVitie shook his head. "He'll have enough on his plate. Don't press him too hard, Jim."

Taggart pushed his chair back and stood up. He faced McVitie warily. "There's one other thing, sir."

"What is it?"

"I want to pull Eleanor Samson in for questioning."

McVitie was silent for a while, thinking. "I see. Reasonable grounds?"

"Very," Taggart nodded emphatically. "I have a reliable witness who saw her in a heated argument with the King girl shortly before the fire broke out. And jealousy is the oldest motive in the world."

McVitie pondered some more, then looked into Taggart's eyes. "Why did you tell me? You don't need permission to do your job."

Taggart faced him squarely. "You involved yourself in this case, sir. I'm keeping you abreast of the situation."

McVitie identified the root cause of Taggart's underlying antagonism. It had been niggling at him all day. "I'm not watching your back, Jim, if that's what you think."

It was out in the open now.

"No?" Taggart said, doubtingly. "Not seeing how an old street copper shapes up against one of the bright new whizz kids? Marking a few cards for future use?"

McVitie was getting angry. He resented Taggart's implications. It was time for a few home truths. He restrained his temper, keeping his voice cool. "Of course you're an old street cop, Jim. One of the best. And young Livingstone is bright, and brash, and over-eager . . . and all the other things which go with youth and inexperience. Good God, man . . . why the hell do you think we put you two together?"

Taggart took a few moments to digest McVitie's little speech. He recognised the compliment his superior had paid him . . . but he was damned if he was going to let him know it. "So I'm on special training duty now, am I?" he demanded, petulantly.

McVitie saw through the bluster. He'd known Jim Taggart too long. "Look — this is your case, Jim . . . you conduct it as you see fit. Just one thing . . . and accept that it's a personal observation, not advice. I don't think you can treat Eleanor Samson like any old suspect. She's a celebrity . . . a star. You'll have media interest to contend with. Kid gloves . . . know what I mean?"

"Don't you mean white gloves," Taggart said sarcastically. "I thought we were policemen, not opera lovers."

McVitie shrugged gently. "I'd like to think we can also be gentlemen."

"Suggesting that I'm not."

"I didn't say that, Jim."

Taggart laughed out loud. He felt good now that the air had been cleared. "No, I know you didn't sir. You didn't have to."

Taggart continued to feel cheery all the way to the hospital. So he was supposed to rub down a few of young Livingstone's sharp edges, was he? Now *there* was a purpose in life!

Mulholland was propped up in bed. An oxygen mask lay on the pillow beside him. A senior nurse stood by in attendance, ready to use it if necessary. Taggart and Livingstone stood beside the bed.

"Tell us what happened, Mr Mulholland," Taggart prompted.

Mulholland's ashen face screwed up with the memory. "It was just after Doctor MacNaughton had left," he recalled. "I smelled burning. I looked out of the workshop window and saw smoke billowing up the back garden. By the time I got to the front door the whole boat was ablaze. Thick black smoke everywhere. I looked for Kirsty . . ." The old man broke off and looked up at Taggart, his eyes pleading. "Is she . . . ?"

Mulholland didn't have to finish the question. The look on Taggart's face gave him the answer. "I tried to save her . . . I tried." His voice tailed off weakly.

"Did you see your daughter?" Taggart asked.

Mulholland looked surprised. "Eleanor left the house nearly an hour before. She and John had words. She went off in a huff."

"We believe she came back," Taggart said flatly, studying the old man's face for reaction. There was none. Mulholland merely looked confused.

"We need to talk to your daughter, Mr Mulholland," Livingstone said. "Do you have any idea where she went?"

Mulholland shook his head slowly.

"Do you know where we might find her?" Taggart asked.

Mulholland appeared to be struggling to remember something. "What time is it?"

Livingstone glanced at his watch. "Nearly five o'clock."

"She had an evening rehearsal call . . . with the opera company," Mulholland volunteered. "Six-thirty, I believe. The Highfield rehearsal rooms."

"Thank you." Taggart nudged Livingstone, jerking his head towards the door.

Outside in the corridor, Livingstone looked surprised. "What's the rush? We've got an hour and a half yet."

"Andrews is coming in with the autopsy report," Taggart informed him. "I want everything to hand before I confront Eleanor Samson. Besides, I want a wee word with Alison while I'm here." Taggart dug in his pocket and pulled out his car keys. He tossed them to Livingstone. "Here . . . bring the car round to the main entrance. I'll be there in three minutes."

Taggart strode off down the corridor. Livingstone watched his back, tossing the bunch of keys thoughtfully in his palm. He wondered whether Alison would tell her father about their meeting, and what his reaction would be. That was the worst thing about working with Taggart. Never knowing what his reaction was going to be.

Andrews dropped a thin dossier onto Taggart's desk.

"Not the most pleasant job," he commented.

Taggart looked up at him with a sardonic smile. "You get *pleasant* ones?"

Andrews ignored him. He turned to Livingstone. "Well, you were right, young man. One of those lacerations *was* a stab wound. It penetrated the floor of the skull and went all the way to the lower medulla."

"Which is where?" Taggart asked.

Livingstone tapped the back of his neck. "The section of the brain where it joins the spinal cord."

Taggart glared at him. "Weapon?" he asked Andrews.

"I'd say you were looking for a blade of at least six-and-a-half inches long. Thin, single cutting edge."

"So she was dead before the fire started?" Livingstone asked.

"Very. Hardly any carbon monoxide in the blood. No soot particles in the lungs. Have you had the fire report yet?"

Taggart nodded. "Definitely arson."

"To make it look like an accident, no doubt," Andrews paused, frowning. "Strange."

"How?" Taggart asked.

"Skilful killing . . . clumsy cover-up," Andrews observed. "Strikes me as a bit odd, that's all."

Livingstone was intrigued. "But couldn't the stab wound have been a fluke . . . a wild lunge that got lucky?"

"Lucky for the killer, you mean? Yes, indeed it could. I must admit I had not considered that possibility."

"And how much force would be required to deliver such a wound?"

"Oh, not a great deal. The blade surpassed most of the muscle tissue. Mostly soft flesh in that area. The assailant wouldn't have to be a very strong man, if that's what you're getting at."

"Or woman," Taggart put in.

"Or woman. Indeed," Andrews agreed.

"Right!" Taggart jumped to his feet. "Let's go get her, Peter. And thank you, Doctor Andrews."

"Her?" Andrews queried softly.

"Eleanor Samson."

Andrews raised his eyebrows. "The singer? Fine voice."

"Well let's hope she uses it to give us a quick confession," Taggart muttered. "We might just wrap this one up in record time."

"So . . . what did you find to talk about?" Taggart said, suddenly. He and Livingstone were sitting in the car, outside the rehearsal rooms.

Livingstone was mystified.

"You and Alison," Taggart went on. "Your little *tête a tête* with my daughter when you were supposed to be on duty outside Mulholland's room."

"They knew where to find me," Livingstone muttered, on the defensive.

"Aye . . . somewhere between the canteen and the social club.

Chatting up my daughter." He studied Livingstone's face for a moment. "Funny, I wouldn't have thought you were Alison's type. She usually goes for the macho, action-man image."

It was a savage put-down. Livingstone might have responded, but a Mercedes sports car had just pulled into a parking space in front of them. Eleanor Samson climbed out.

"Let's go," Taggart said. He was out of the car and at Eleanor's side before she had locked her car door.

Eleanor gave a nervous start as she straightened up to find him there. Fright gave way to anger. "Who are you? What do you want?"

Taggart flashed his ID card. "Police officers, Mrs Samson. We'd like to question you about a death which took place earlier today."

"Death?" Eleanor repeated the word without comprehension.

Taggart studied her eyes. She looked shocked and confused. Taggart reminded himself that opera singers took drama training. "Kirsty King," he snapped out. Again, he watched her eyes for a flicker of emotion. There was a glint of . . . something. Taggart couldn't identify it. He was unprepared for her physical reaction.

Eleanor drew in a slow, deep breath. She straightened up, pulling back her shoulders and pushing out her chest. For a second, Taggart thought she was going to burst into song. The stance was one of hauteur. Eleanor's face screwed up into a look of disdain. It was a pose Taggart recognised. It was arrogance. He had seen it at their first meeting and disliked the woman at once. That feeling was reinforced now.

"You really must excuse me. I have a rehearsal," Eleanor said casually. It was as if death, policemen, the law . . . all such things were matters of concern to a lower order of beings.

Taggart was momentarily taken aback as she pushed past him and went to walk away. His anger broke. "Mrs Samson!" Taggart spat her name out with vehemence.

Eleanor stopped, turned. The haughty expression faded, replaced by uncertainty, perhaps even a tinge of fright. The look of someone who knows they have just met their match.

Taggart jabbed his thumb towards his car. Meekly, silently, Eleanor walked towards it. Livingstone opened the door for her.

The interview room was small and sparsely furnished. A desk, two chairs. Eleanor shuddered affectedly as she was shown into it.

"I hate small rooms."

"A phobia?" Livingstone enquired solicitously.

"No . . . just a preference." Eleanor's eyes were on Taggart as she spoke, a thin, mirthless smile on her lips.

Taggart felt his guts tighten. She'd recovered her composure — with a vengeance. She'd found his weakness now, and she'd play on it.

Eleanor seated herself without an invitation. "I believe I am entitled to a telephone call?"

Taggart nodded, his teeth gritted. "That is your right."

"Then perhaps you would be good enough to have someone make it for me. I would like to let my company know why I am late for rehearsal."

Again that superior, taunting smile. Taggart faced it impassively, refusing to let the woman get through to him. He glanced up at Livingstone, gesturing with his eyes. Livingstone went out to make the call.

"We met this morning," Eleanor said. "You were with your wife at the concert."

It could have been polite social chit-chat. The smile, showing off her undeniably attractive face could have been genuine. The way she sat in the chair could have been the natural grace of a woman used to public performance.

Taggart was needled. Could he be wrong? Could his deep, ingrained sense of prejudice be clouding his judgement? Perhaps it was all imagined; the arrogance, the sneering condescension, the reference to his wife with the implied adjective 'crippled'. The woman's attitude was throwing him, distracting him from his job. Perhaps intentionally so. Taggart couldn't afford to play the complicated mind games Eleanor Samson was so adept at. There was only one way to play things. Hard. Straight. The only way he knew.

"We'll need the suit you're wearing. For forensic examination."

"You'd like me to strip off?"

Now Taggart knew she was taunting him. "We'll fetch you something else to wear."

"All my clothes are at my father's house."

"We'll send someone," Taggart said.

38

"Someone with a bit of taste, I hope."

Taggart could fight the urge no longer. He needed to hit out at her, smash through the facade and reach something vulnerable, real. "Talking of your father . . . I ought to tell you he's in hospital."

He'd got through. Taggart saw alarm on her face and didn't feel very proud of himself.

"Why? What's wrong with him?"

"He was trying to put out a fire," Taggart said.

The bluster was gone, suddenly. The was just a grown-up little girl worried about her daddy. For the first time, Taggart had real doubts. Even an actress couldn't fake a look like that. He'd seen it so many times, over so many years. In Alison's eyes.

"He's all right. He's recovering," Taggart needed to reassure her, for his own sake.

"I want to see him."

"I'm afraid that's not possible . . . for the moment," Taggart said gently.

Eleanor's eyes blazed. She stood, slamming her palms on the surface of the desk. "Who do you think you are, telling me I can't see my own father?"

The barriers were up again. Taggart sighed. "I'm a policeman, Mrs Samson," he reminded her.

The interview room door opened. Livingstone popped his head in. He gave Taggart a silent message. Taggart walked to the door, stepped outside into the passage. Livingstone whispered, "The opera company are sending a solicitor. They insisted. I've been instructed to tell Mrs Samson not to talk to us until he arrives."

Taggart clenched his fist, shaking it in the air. "Aw, great!," he hissed, frustrated. McVitie's earlier words came back to him. "We don't make the rules, Jim. Just follow them."

Taggart simmered down, remembering. Justice wielded a two-edged sword.

The interview room had been furnished with three more chairs, making it even more cramped. Eleanor had changed into a neat fawn two-piece which accentuated her imposing figure. She was seated at the desk as Taggart and Livingstone walked in. James Donaldson, the solicitor, sat beside her. Taggart recognised him, with a slight sinking feeling. They'd crossed swords before.

Donaldson was good.

Donaldson took the initiative. He stood, facing Taggart squarely. He too remembered previous encounters — and Taggart's head-down, bull-at-a-gate interrogation methods. "Chief Inspector Taggart? James Donaldson. I've had a chance to talk to my client and she is now ready to answer your questions. So if you would like to proceed . . ."

"That's very good of you," Taggart said, with heavy sarcasm. He pulled a chair away from the desk towards the wall and sat down. Livingstone continued standing.

Eleanor looked at the younger man, a clever, little-girl-lost smile on her face. "How is my father?"

"Making a fine recovery, Mrs Samson. There's no need for concern."

"Thank you." Eleanor was especially polite. Taggart assumed it was for his benefit.

Taggart addressed himself to Eleanor, though he kept half an eye on Donaldson, not sure how far the man would let him go.

"Let's get straight to the point, shall we? You were seen arguing with Kirsty King by the boat in your father's drive shortly before the fire started."

"Seen? By whom?" Eleanor demanded.

"Do you deny it?" Taggart pounced. One lie, and he had the start of a prosecution case.

"No," Eleanor said. There was defiance in her voice.

"What time did you leave her?"

Eleanor shrugged carelessly. "How should I remember? I spoke to her for five minutes, that's all."

"What was the argument about?"

The superior, almost pitying smile. Such a naive question. "She was trying to take my husband away from me."

Livingstone spoke for the first time. "But you have been separated for six years, Mrs Samson."

Eleanor turned her scorn on him. "He is still my husband."

Possessive, Livingstone thought. Aggressively so. But enough for murder? "Where did you go after you left her?"

"I drove up into the hills. I found a very quiet lane. I parked my car, sat back . . . and had a very long cry."

"Alone?" Taggart demanded.

That smile again. "I'm not in the habit of crying in company,

Inspector."

It was time to take the gloves off, Taggart thought. To hell with McVitie. "Did you kill Kirsty King?"

Donaldson shifted forward in his chair. "Really, Inspector."

Taggart ignored him. He repeated the question, more aggressively. "I'll ask you again. Did you kill Kirsty King?"

Eleanor's face was drained of emotion. "No, I did not."

Taggart was into his stride now, and nothing was going to stop him. Denials, solicitors, pussy-footing Chief Superintendents . . . He slammed his clenched fist down on to the desk. "Oh, yes. You killed her, Mrs Samson. You killed Kirsty King and then you started a fire to destroy the evidence."

Donaldson was shaken. He had never seen Taggart so intensely committed. It was more than certainty. It was almost . . . hate. He retreated to a defensive position. "I really must protest, Inspector. I assume you have some evidence to back up these wild allegations?"

He could have been speaking into thin air. Taggart's blazing eyes were riveted on Eleanor Samson. "Don't you realise that you could have killed your father as well?"

Donaldson jumped to his feet angrily, pushed to the limit. "That question assumes my client has already admitted one murder. Out of order, don't you think? I really am not prepared to be a party to these bullying tactics a moment longer. I must ask you now, Inspector Taggart . . . are you prepared to lay formal charges against my client?"

Taggart slumped back in his chair. It was over. "No, not at this moment. We do, however, reserve the right to question her again."

"Then perhaps you will contact me when the time comes." Donaldson was already helping Eleanor out of her chair. He steered her towards the door.

Taggart leaned forward, propping his elbows on the desk and cradling his chin on his hands. He fumed silently.

Eleanor reached the door and allowed Donaldson to open it for her. From behind, Livingstone spoke in a quiet, calm voice. "The evidence was not destroyed in the fire, Mrs Samson. We know exactly how Kirsty died."

Eleanor whirled round, regarding him, seeing the subtle, confident smile she knew so well. Doubt flickered across her eyes as she reassessed him. Not, as she had first thought, a mere foil to Taggart's bluster. In his own, quiet way, Livingstone was as menacing as his superior.

Livingstone held her eyes for a timeless moment. Then, at Donaldson's prompting, Eleanor turned away and allowed herself to be ushered out through the door.

Graeme waited for her outside the police station. He watched Donaldson take his leave and then ran across to greet her.

Eleanor gave her son a tired smile. "Oh, it's good to see you, Graeme. How did you know I was here?"

"They told me at the rehearsal rooms. I came to meet you." Graeme looked at her with a worried expression. "It's all about Kirsty, isn't it?"

Eleanor nodded, "Yes." She linked her arm in his and started walking. "Come on. We'll go and pick up my car and go to Uncle Don's for the night. I couldn't face going back to Grandad's house . . . not now."

They walked in silence for a few minutes. Then Graeme stopped, abruptly, fixing her with a serious stare. "I know you didn't kill her, Mum. But even if you had . . . it wouldn't matter. She deserved to die."

Eleanor looked at her son curiously. His eyes glinted with the same inner hate which she had seen earlier in the day. She didn't understand, but she was too tired to pursue it.

Chapter Five

BRENNAN packed his camera case with three extra rolls of film and a set of daylight filters. It was only eight-thirty in the morning, but it promised to be a bright, sunny day. He wanted to make the most of the morning before his lunchtime stint behind the bar.

He peered cautiously out into the public bar. Olive MacQueen, the part-time help was busy cleaning the liquor shelves. Of Lilly, there was no sign. Brennan crept through the bar, heading for the door.

"And where do you think you're off to?" Lilly's hated voice yelped out from the foot of the stairs behind him.

Brennan stopped in his tracks, caught like a thief. He turned, forcing a smile. "Just thought I'd get out for an hour or so," he muttered.

"Well you'll no' go empty-handed," Lilly snapped. "I've a few errands for you to run. You wait there." Lilly disappeared back up the stairs. When she reappeared, she had a pile of clothes over one arm and a shopping list in her hand. "Drop these into the dry-cleaners . . . and you can get these things from the supermarket on your way home. And no stopping in Jackie's bar, Keith Brennan. Don't think I don't know when you come in here reeking of polo mints."

Brennan took the clothes and the list. He slunk out, his morning dampened by that old and familiar resentment eating him up inside. Behind him, the two women got into the perennial conversation regarding the frailties of menfolk.

"It's no the drinking you have to worry about," Olive observed. "It's when they start going into the betting shop."

"Aye . . . well my Keith had better not ever start *that*. We've little enough money as it is."

"Talking of money — can you use me any more this week, Lilly? I can always do with the little extra, you know?"

"I'll see what I can do," Lilly promised her.

Brennan paused outside the dry-cleaning shop. He looked at his reflection in the window, combing his hair carefully. Satisfied with his appearance, he stepped into the shop, smiling.

Dorothy Milner was the sort of woman any man would want to look his best for. Just a year short of her thirtieth birthday, she had the enviable blend of youthful attractiveness and sophisticated maturity. It was a potent mixture. Many men before Keith Brennan had fallen under its spell.

"Morning," Brennan said, brightly. He dumped Lilly's dresses across the counter top. "And how are we this fine new day?"

Dorothy struck a provocative pose. "My — aren't we the chirpy one this morning?

"All the better for seeing you," Brennan said, and it wasn't just a come-on.

Dorothy took the clothes, tagged them and handed Brennan his call-slip. She eyed his camera bag. "And what are we photographing today?"

"Oh — architecture, places of interest . . . that sort of thing."

"Oh, yes?" Dorothy's eyes flashed. She managed to make the two simple words into a complete flirtation routine. "I'd have thought a man like you would have been into glamour photography."

Brennan preened under the subtle flattery. "I've had my moments, you know?"

Dorothy leaned across the counter. Brennan could see the swell of her breasts down the cleavage of her light blouse. "I'll bet you have," she said in a soft, seductive voice.

The shop door opened behind Brennan with a sharp ping. Dorothy straightened up quickly, becoming business-like for the new customer. Brennan cursed his luck. He waved the tickets in his hand. "See you tomorrow, then."

"Yes. Thank you, sir." He was just another customer.

Brennan had a spring in his step again. Thoughts of the dreaded Lilly were pushed back into a dark corner of his mind. His thoughts now were of Dorothy, in a setting where his imagination could run riot.

A proper photographic studio — lights, backdrops, a battery of the world's finest cameras and lenses at his fingertips. Dorothy standing on a podium, slipping a light housecoat away from her smooth, bare shoulders. Her naked body glowing under the light and heat of strategically placed floods. Posing . . . for him.

The clattering of an old tin can snapped him back to reality. Two kids were kicking the can across a patch of waste ground in an impromptu game of football. With something of a start, Brennan took in his surroundings, orientating himself. Somehow, in the course of his daydream, he had managed to wander right through the main shopping centre and into the redevelopment housing area over a mile outside it. Old city — struggling to come to terms with the broken promises and the unfinished dreams of the past decade.

The inner-city village concept, the planners had so proudly called it. Green parks, playing fields, surrounded by small and cosy non-geometric clusters of modern houses. Built to house the refugees from the other slum areas of the city, when the rotting tenements and the claustrophobic terraces crashed down to make way for the new factories.

But there were no new factories, and many of the old ones were closed and derelict. So the area remained frozen in transition, waiting for the fast-fading dream of a new economic boom. And two small kids kicked a tin can over a patch of rubble where the sports and leisure centre should have been.

Brennan was not an overly sensitive man, yet the place positively vibrated with a strange, morbid fascination which was hard to resist. It seemed to call out to be recorded, captured forever on a roll of film. Without fully understanding why, Brennan pulled the Nikon from his camera case, set it on automatic and began to sweep the area, firing off shot after shot.

Jimmy Petrie was one of life's losers. At the tender age of eighteen, he had already accepted this terrible fact. He had never had a job, and was never likely to. His schooling had been minimal, his qualifications nil. No-one had ever cared enough to guide him towards a better future. Father unknown, mother alcoholic. Petrie was on the streets at fifteen, learning how to survive.

Stealing was the easiest way. It always had been. From the first penny gobstopper to the first tube of glue, Petrie had taken those things which made life tolerable, and which nobody else would provide. Now it was hard cash. Cash bought beer, the chance of a big win in the betting shop, or a handful of the pills two black guys sold outside Maryhill Secondary School.

His main source of revenue was telephone kiosks. The cash

boxes were fairly easy to prise open, they usually contained at least a fiver and they provided him with a specific outlet for his burning sense of injustice. Petrie hated British Telecom, ever since the publicity surrounding the privatisation sell-off had made him aware of it. He hated the idea that a company could make profits of figures beyond his comprehension. He hated the fact that it had thousands of men in well-paid jobs whilst he was on the dole. Most of all, he hated the idea that ordinary people had been able to buy shares in this incredible wealth. The only thing Jimmy Petrie had ever had shares in was a packet of cigarettes.

He had chosen his latest target carefully. It was fairly isolated, near a patch of waste ground. There was a housing development not too far away, so the phone obviously got used. Petrie looked around cautiously before entering the kiosk. There was no-one around likely to cause him any trouble. Just two kids kicking a can around, and some stupid old geezer taking photographs. He stepped into the telephone box and slid a thin, long-bladed knife from under his jerkin. He began to tackle the lock on the coin-box.

Brennan continued to take photographs, unaware that a drama was unfolding behind his back. As Petrie was intent on his crime, a yellow Telecom van was approaching, on a routine service.

The van stopped on the blind side of the telephone box. The service engineer climbed out, tool-box in his hand. He started to walk towards the kiosk.

Brennan began to pan round in a circle, checking that he had not missed anything remotely worth photographing. A flash of red in the viewfinder caught his attention. Brennan stopped moving, watching the telephone box just as the engineer came level with the glass and caught Petrie in the act.

Brennan saw what was coming. He fingered the automatic zoom and the drama leapt into close-up. It happened in a matter of a few furious seconds, yet to Brennan, watching through the static eye of his camera, it seemed almost like slow-motion. He pressed the shutter release regularly, catching every major incident. The engineer yanking open the door. His hand on Petrie's arm, pulling him outside. Petrie struggling to free himself. Petrie's arm coming free, swinging back, holding the knife. The engineer kicking out, desperately in an attempt to catch the youth in the groin. Petrie's equally desperate lunge forward with the outstretched knife, trying to hold the man at bay. The engineer mistiming the kick, losing his balance. Toppling forward, tripping over his own outstretched leg, falling on to the blade.

Brennan's camera captured it all, along with the look of agony on the engineer's face as the blade slid in under his ribs. Petrie's face . . . a close-up study in horror. Then a running figure, leaving behind a wounded man and a small envelope which had fallen from his pocket during the affray.

Brennan stood in a daze of disbelief. Slowly, he lowered the camera and tried to force his mind and body into action. It seemed to take an age before he could make his feet move, run towards the telephone box and snatch up the receiver.

He dialled 999 in a dream. There was something crowding in the back of his mind, something more powerful than reality. The operator's voice came over the line. "Emergency . . . what service do you require, please?"

Suddenly, Brennan knew what that something was. He was calm and alert. His brain was functioning with cool precision.

"Ambulance," he said crisply, and gave the location of the phone kiosk. Then he dropped the receiver, letting it dangle on the end of the cord. Stepping outside, he picked up the envelope which the fleeing youth had dropped. It was a dole cheque.

Taggart and Livingstone waited in a small vestibule adjoining the school assembly hall. A side door opened, and Graeme Samson entered.

"I was told you wanted to see me."

"Graeme Samson. We're police officers," Taggart said. "We'd like to ask you some questions."

"Can I see your identification, please?"

Taggart was ruffled. He wasn't used to having his authority questioned by 18-year-olds. Nevertheless, the boy was within his rights. Irritably, Taggart drew out his ID card and held it up quickly. Graeme reached out, took it from his fingers and examined it closely before offering it back.

"Satisfied, are you? Everything in order, is it?" Taggart's tone was caustic.

The youngster was unimpressed. "We're told you can't be too careful these days."

Taggart glowered. "Let's go for a walk outside."

47

A few moments later, they were strolling in the private school's extensive grounds. Taggart and Livingstone fell into Graeme's pace, either side of him. "We hear you were a naughty boy yesterday," Taggart said.

If he had hoped to throw the boy off balance, he failed. Graeme looked across poker-faced. "Really. What did I do?"

"You disappeared after the school rugby match. You were supposed to come back for a maths tutorial. You didn't."

Graeme merely shrugged.

"Where did you go, Graeme?" Livingstone put in gently, thinking that the lad might respond to him better. He was wrong.

"So — I skived off school for an afternoon. Big deal."

"Let's get down to specifics," Taggart said in a slightly raised voice. "Where were you between the hours of twelve noon and two p.m.?"

Graeme's face registered an amused smile. "Good Lord . . . I thought the police only asked questions like that in the old movies." He became serious. "I went for a long walk, down by the River Kelvin."

"Can anyone vouch for that?"

"No, why should anyone?"

"Why did you skive off, Graeme?" Livingstone tried again.

The boy laughed. "Who needs a reason?"

"Girlfriend, was it? A little bit of nicey-naughties in the bushes."

Graeme started to blush. "No . . . nothing like that."

"Have you got a girlfriend, Graeme?" Livingstone asked.

"No." The word came out almost in a whisper.

"Why are you blushing?" Taggart demanded.

The boy seemed rattled for the first time. He stammered slightly. "I . . . I don't know."

"How did you feel about your father and Kirsty King?" Taggart hit him with the real question, while he was off balance.

Graeme's face set into a hard mask. "She was what he wanted."

"And how about you? Fancy her, did you?"

Graeme shook his head forcefully. *Too* forcefully, Taggart thought. "No."

"Did you think she was an attractive girl, then?"

"I don't know," Graeme shrugged and tried to look vague.

Taggart stopped in his stride. He reached out and gripped

Graeme by the shoulder, roughly. He thrust his free hand a few inches in front of the boy's face. "How many fingers am I holding up?"

"Five."

Taggart let him go. "Well, you're not blind, are you?"

"Look, can I go now? I have exams in a few weeks time."

"Didn't seem to matter yesterday," Livingstone reminded him.

"That was maths. My tutor says I'm a near-genius in mathematics."

Taggart had had enough. He gestured with his thumb. "Go on, clear off, near-genius."

The boy turned and ran off.

"He's hiding something," Taggart muttered.

"Cheeky little bastard, too," Livingstone observed.

Taggart didn't seem to have heard the comment. Then, a few seconds later, he turned on Livingstone as if with a sudden thought. "You know . . . I imagine you were a lot like that at school."

Livingstone glared at him. "One day, you'll try to put me down just once too often."

Taggart began to laugh quietly. "Oh, I don't try, Peter. I don't try."

Chapter Six

MULHOLLAND was sitting up in bed reading a magazine as Doctor MacNaughton came in.

"Morning, Frank. How are you feeling?"

Mulholland dropped the magazine over the side of the bed. He forced a weak smile. "Well, my heart stood up. Maybe I will in a couple of days. You're sure my heart isn't more like an elderly cat? Nine lives?"

MacNaughton smiled back. "A couple of days rest, and we'll talk about getting you out of here. Have you seen Eleanor?"

Mulholland's smile faded. "Aye. She came. John too. And the police, asking questions."

"They came to see me as well. I was even treated as a suspect — because I was there."

"What do you think?" Mulholland looked wretched. "I have to know."

MacNaughton shook his head slowly. "It's not what I think, Frank. It's what the police make of it. I only told them what I saw."

"You know they suspect Eleanor?"

MacNaughton nodded. "It was to be expected. I saw them arguing, Frank. Eleanor had a motive."

Mulholland let out a long, deep sigh which moaned in his throat. Old wounds were opening, the pain they had caused undiminished. "It changes everything. Makes a mockery . . ."

"Don't let it prey on your mind, Frank," MacNaughton interrupted. "You need rest, relaxation."

The advice went unheeded.

"Not that I ever felt close to her," Mulholland went on. "But now this . . ." His voice tailed off. He sank back into his pillows, loooking up at MacNaughton. There was a strange look in his eyes. A pleading for forgiveness, more suited to a priest than a doctor. "Am I wrong? To feel how I do?"

MacNaughton looked embarrassed. It wasn't a question he could answer. "It was forty years ago, Frank."

"Aye," Mulholland sighed again. "The trouble is, I just can't forget." He turned his head into the pillow, feeling suddenly weary.

MacNaughton watched him silently, until sleep came. He crept out of the room, closing the door quietly behind him.

The desk sergeant waved an envelope in the air as Taggart and Livingstone walked into the station.

"Lab report you were waiting for, sir. And Superintendent McVitie would like to see you."

Livingstone detoured to pick up the report, tearing the envelope open as he followed Taggart towards McVitie's office.

Taggart stopped outside the door, letting Livingstone catch up. He held out his hand for the report. "Anything?"

Livingstone said nothing, but handed the papers over with something of a triumphant flourish. Taggart glanced through the report quickly, keeping a perfectly straight face for his colleague's benefit. Livingstone looked slightly disappointed as Taggart tapped on the Super's door and walked in without waiting for an answer.

"What have we got, Jim?" McVitie asked, dourly.

Taggart tapped the lab report with his finger. "Three separate petrol splashes on the front of Eleanor Samson's trousers. All recent."

McVitie perked up. "Octane rating?"

"They were only vapours," Livingstone put in. "They need a bucketful of the stuff before they can test for grade."

"Pity," McVitie was deflated again. "If we could prove it was the same grade as that used on the boat . . ."

"Nothing there, either," Taggart said. "The can was evaporated out; hoses washed out any other traces."

McVitie was silent for a while, pondering. Finally, he addressed them both. "So we haven't got much at all. Your suggestions, gentlemen?"

Taggart opened his mouth to speak, but Livingstone beat him to it. "I say pull her in again . . . quickly, while she's still rattled," he suggested brightly. "Confront her with the petrol stains on the suit, and force a quick confession."

Taggart pulled his face into an extravagant expression of mock amazement, making sure that both McVitie and Livingstone saw it. "As simple as that. Now why didn't I think of it?"

Livingstone coloured slightly, partly from embarrassment, partly from anger.

McVitie was not amused, either. "He has a point, Jim. An early confession would be nice. I'd like this one as quick and clean as possible. The Press are already on to us."

Taggart shrugged, annoyed that his attempt at sarcasm had fallen flat. "Whatever you say, sir. We'll try it the whizz-kid way."

Livingstone wasn't taking anything — not with McVitie on his side. "And I've got one more suggestion to make," he said firmly. "We forget that she's Eleanor Samson."

Brennan came out of his darkroom, more than pleased with his morning's work. The photographs had turned out better than expected. He wondered, momentarily, how much a national newspaper might pay for them. The idea was rejected immediately. They were worth far more than any offer of mere money.

He tiptoed down the stairs and peered into the bar. Olive stood behind the counter with her back to him, smoking a cigarette. The place was virtually empty, with just one drunk sleeping peacefully in a corner. There was no sign of Lilly, as Brennan had hoped. A creature of rigid habit, she always took an after-lunch nap when things got quiet, usually leaving him to clear up and do the glasses. Luckily, it was one of Olive's odd half-days. There was nothing to stop him getting out.

Just to check, Brennan crept into the small parlour behind the bar. He poked his head round the door. Lilly lay out on the scruffy day-bed, sleeping goggles over her eyes, mouth slackly open, snoring. The sight disgusted him. With a renewed sense of purpose, he let himself out through the back door and skirted round the yard to the car. He climbed in and drove off, to keep a very important appointment.

Depite Donaldson's presence, Eleanor was ill at ease. Her blue trouser suit lay out on the interview room table, a mute accuser. For the first time, she felt a real sense of threat. Yesterday's sense of unreality, of playing some bizarre game, had faded. Eleanor realised now that the police were intent on pinning a murder charge on her — and that they were serious about it.

Their change of tactics had confused her even further. She had come in expecting Taggart to launch into the attack with his bullying attitude. Instead, he had greeted her silently, retired into a corner of the room and sat there ever since, a thin, distant smile on his face. It was Livingstone, previously quiet and mild-mannered, who now had the aggressive attitude, bombarding her with questions until her head reeled. Even so, there was no let-up.

"We're still waiting, Mrs Samson. These petrol splashes," Livingstone prompted.

Eleanor gave a faint shrug. "They must have come from when I was filling my car. Yesterday morning."

"What time?"

Eleanor dithered, waving her hands distractedly. "After I left my father's house . . . I have no idea of the exact time."

"You said nothing about stopping at a garage yesterday," Livingstone accused. "Yet we went through your movements half a dozen times. A strange thing to forget, wouldn't you say . . . under the circumstances?"

"It didn't seem important enough to mention at the time," Eleanor muttered, weakly.

Livingstone sneered. "Not important? A girl is burned to a cinder in a fire started with petrol, and you think incriminating evidence is not important?"

Donaldson was far from happy with the way the interview was going. "Perhaps you could choose your words with more care, Detective Sergeant," he interposed. "I hardly think that petrol stains are in themselves incriminating."

Livingstone ignored him. He was well into his stride now, he was sure he had Eleanor on the run. Now was the time to try his bluff. "You drive a Mercedes, don't you, Mrs Samson?"

Eleanor nodded, "Yes."

"Which takes four-star petrol, no doubt?"

Eleanor nodded again, "Yes." She didn't quite understand where this latest line of questioning was heading.

Livingstone pounced. "The petrol used to start the fire on the boat was two-star. Just like the stains on your suit." He kept his eyes fiercely fixed on hers, in an accusatory stare. Now was the moment. She *had* to crack now.

Livingstone was disappointed. Eleanor merely looked confused. "I . . . I wouldn't know," she murmured, uncertainly.

Donaldson jumped in to her rescue. "Surely the petrol had

evaporated?"

Livingstone kept up the bluff. "The vapour still remained."

Donaldson smiled to himself. "I wasn't aware that octane rating could be determined from a vapour trace. Unless there has been some recent and dramatic breakthrough in forensic science."

Livingstone felt all his self-confidence ebbing away. His bluff had been called and he'd lost the game. In desperation, he glanced over at Taggart, a silent plea in his eyes. Taggart remained mute, still smiling infuriatingly. He was wondering how Livingstone was going to wriggle off the hook he had impaled himself upon.

Livingstone didn't even try. "Which garage did you stop at, Mrs Samson?" he asked in a quiet, calm voice.

"I can't remember the name. An Esso station, I believe. On the road by my son's school."

Livingstone stood up. He stalked from the room, giving Taggart a disgusted stare as he passed.

"He's very keen," Donaldson said to Taggart.

The smile on Taggart's face snapped off like an extinguished light. All the aggression was there again. It had always been there, lurking behind the disarming smile. Let Donaldson and Eleanor have no doubts — it wasn't over yet. "Aye . . . he's keen," Taggart agreed. "Because that's the way I taught him."

Brennan waited in his car, opposite the block of flats where Jimmy Petrie lived. He had been there nearly two hours already, but remained calmly patient. He'd waited so many years . . . what was another hour or so?

An early edition of the local paper lay on the passenger seat. 'Telecom Engineer Critical' the headline declared. Brennan glanced down at it for the hundreth time, revelling in the sensation it gave him. That, and the photographs in his pocket, gave him a feeling he hadn't known for years. Power.

His patience was finally rewarded. Through the side window he saw Petrie emerge from the block, cut across the tarmac surround and head off down the street. Brennan checked one of the photographs, to make sure there was no mistake. Then he started the car, did a U-turn in the road and began to cruise after the youth.

Overtaking him, Brennan drove on for twenty yards, stopped and climbed out of the car. Crossing round the front of the car,

Brennan leaned casually back against the front wing, his feet on the pavement. He waited until the youth was almost abreast of him. "Jimmy Petrie?"

The boy stopped, his attitude at once guarded and aggressive. "What's it tae you?"

"I've got something of yours," Brennan said. He pulled the dole cheque from his pocket. "You *are* Jimmy Petrie, are you?"

Petrie saw the envelope, recognised it. "Aye." He reached out, snatching it from Brennan's fingers. Only then did realisation dawn. His eyes narrowed, a nervous twitch tugged at the corner of his mouth. The aggression was gone, suddenly, replaced by uncertainty. "Where did you find this?"

"By the phone box," Brennan said quietly. He reached in through the open car window and pulled out the newspaper, showing Petrie the headline. "It looks like he might die."

For a moment, Petrie braced himself as though to run, then thought better of it. He curled his lips in a gesture of defiance. "You're not the polis . . . who *are* you?"

"Just a man who likes to take photographs," Brennan said easily. "Would you like to see one?" Without waiting for an answer, he pulled a print from his pocket and extended it. It showed the knife just beginning to pierce the engineer's chest. Petrie's face was clearly visible.

Petrie snatched the print, staring at it in disbelief. His fingers trembled. "What you going tae do with this? You'll no' take it to the polis?"

Brennan shrugged. "That depends. You can keep that one, by the way," he added, generously.

Petrie tore the print into several pieces, cramming them in his pocket. He stared at Brennan, looking pleased with himself. Brennan smiled inwardly. As he had expected, the youth was none too bright. "I've got plenty more," Brennan said, producing two more from his pocket to prove it. "And the negatives at home," he added quickly, in case Petrie took it into his head to become violent.

Petrie looked beaten. He adopted a faintly wheedling tone. "Look . . . I didnae mean to hurt that guy. It was an accident. Gissa break, eh? I've already done time."

Brennan didn't believe him. "You're too young to have been inside."

"Borstal. Two years ago," Petrie informed him. "I broke into a shop."

Brennan sucked at his teeth, making vaguely reproving noises. He waved his head slowly from side to side. "Prison's not like Borstal, Jimmy. All the real hard cases. The lifers, sex offenders, child molesters. And the queers, Jimmy . . . they'd love a young lad like you. You'd not have many lonely nights for a long time. Ten . . . maybe twelve years . . . even if you got off with manslaughter."

Petrie shuddered at the thought of it. His eyes narrowed as a thought came to him. "You're nae one of the bastards, are ye? Is that what all this is about?"

Brennan laughed. "No, Jimmy. I'm as straight as you are."

"Then what do you want with me?"

"Just to talk," Brennan said. He opened the car passenger door. "Get in, we'll take a drive."

Brennan walked round the front of the car and climbed in. Petrie hesitated for several seconds, then grudgingly climbed in beside him. They drove off towards the outskirts of the city.

Eleanor and Donaldson were long gone by the time Livingstone returned. He looked dejected.

"Nice try," Taggart said.

Livingstone glared at him angrily. He opened his mouth, about to launch into a bitter tirade. McVitie poked his head into the room, cutting him short.

"So what happened?"

"Her story about the garage holds up," Livingstone admitted morosely. "The cashier remembered the car. Not a lot of Mercedes sports around these parts."

"Which means we have no forensic evidence of any value."

"I'm afraid so, sir."

McVitie turned on Taggart. "That's twice we've had her in here, Jim. Twice she's walked away. How many more times?"

"You were the one who wanted us to act like gentlemen," Taggart reminded him.

The rejoinder had the desired effect. With a quick snort to cover his embarrassment, McVitie withdrew. Taggart addressed Livingstone in a brisk, businesslike manner, making the position clear. He was firmly back in charge, now that the youngster had

had his chance and blown it.

"So . . . we explore further. Find out all you can about Samson's relationship with Kirsty King. Talk to Maxwell the building contractor. I'm going back to the hospital to have another word with Mulholland. Maybe he knows more than he's told us."

"Will you be seeing Alison?" Livingstone asked.

"I might," Taggart glared at him suspiciously. "Why?"

"Could you give her a message?"

"Oh aye . . . what's that?" Taggart felt the hairs prickling on the nape of his neck.

"Just say — 'how about Saturday?' — she'll understand," Livingstone said. He walked off.

Taggart stared after the young man, wrestling with the thoughts of anger and resentment which were suddenly stirred up. Protection . . . or prejudice? Taggart couldn't be sure. Was it just Livingstone . . . or the wider issue about not wanting his daughter to date police officers? And what was he going to do about it?

Chapter Seven

THEY'D told Livingstone that Ted Maxwell was out on site, but given him no idea of the size of the project. Livingstone was impressed. The massive construction area was part of a multi-million pound development scheme. Obviously, Maxwell was a much bigger fish than he had imagined.

Livingstone finally tracked Maxwell down to the perimeter area, deep in discussion with a small group of construction engineers. Livingstone waited patiently until the discussion was finished. Maxwell started to walk away.

"Mr Maxwell?" Livingstone called out.

Maxwell turned, frowning. "Who's asking? And what the hell are you doing on this site without a hard hat?"

Livingstone pulled out his ID. "Police. Detective Sergeant Livingstone."

Maxwell was neither impressed nor apologetic. "What do you want?" he demanded impatiently.

"It's about Kirsty King," Livingstone said.

Maxwell's gruff manner disappeared. He shook his head sadly. "Christine . . . tragic business."

"Can we go somewhere to talk?" Livingstone asked. The background noise of cement mixers, dumper trucks and pneumatic drills was deafening.

Maxwell gestured towards a mobile site office some yards away and walked towards it. Livingstone followed him.

Inside, it was only marginally quieter. Livingstone wondered how any man could live with it, day after day.

Maxwell seated himself at his desk. There wasn't a spare chair. Livingstone stood, looking down on him. "Miss King worked for you before she joined Zeus Property Development, working for John Samson."

"That's right," Maxwell agreed. "So?"

"What did she do?"

Maxwell grinned, "Well she wasn't a hod carrier." He looked up at Livingstone's unsmiling face and changed his tone. "Filing . . . answering the telephone . . . a bit of everything."

Livingstone raised one eyebrow. "Everything?" It was just a hunch.

Maxwell ignored the implication — or chose not to confirm it.

"What sort of girl was she?" Livingstone probed.

"Reliable."

"And her personal life?"

"Exactly that. Personal." Maxwell wasn't giving anything away.

"We *are* trying to find out who murdered her," Livingstone reminded him. "How did you first meet her?"

Maxwell shrugged. "She applied for a job. I took her on. Samson came along, offered her a better deal, she went with him."

"You're saying that your relationship with Miss King was purely on a professional basis?"

Maxwell was guarded. He hesitated momentarily before answering. "I'm saying nothing. I'm just answering your questions."

Livingstone didn't press the point. "Did she have any other boyfriends — besides Samson?"

"None to my knowledge."

"Anyone who might have had a grudge against her?"

"The only person who might have held a grudge against Christine was Eleanor Samson." Maxwell was emphatic. He stood, suddenly. "Look, that's all I can tell you about her. Now I'm a very busy man . . . can I get back to my business?"

There was something too abrupt about his movement. Almost panicky. Livingstone saw worry on Maxwell's face. He followed the man's eyeline down towards his desk. In one of the trays was a colour brochure with a picture of a cabin cruiser on the front. It was identical to the one on which Kirsty King had died. Livingstone took a mental note of the company name: Cumbria Cruisers.

Maxwell scooped up a pile of loose papers and dropped them in to the top of the tray, obscuring the brochure. He wasn't sure whether Livingstone had seen it, or if he had, would make the necessary connection. If that happened, his only other hope was that the police would be too busy with the murder enquiry to follow it up.

Livingstone gave no indication either way. "Well, I think that's all for the time being. Thanks for your help."

Maxwell watched him walk away and silently cursed at himself under his breath. It had been stupid to keep the damned brochure anyway, let alone leave it lying around on his desk.

"Good God! I didn't know places like this still existed." Livingstone looked around the interior of the Firhill Tavern in horror.

Taggart smiled wickedly. He had deliberately nominated the place for their evening meeting, knowing that it would shock the young man. "I suppose you're a fitted carpet and Muzak man?" Taggart said. "Disco lighting and drinks with bits of fruit on top?"

"Bitter," Livingstone said.

"Half?"

"Pint."

Taggart moved in towards the bar to order the drinks. Lilly moved along to serve him. "Evening, Mr Taggart."

"Evening, Lilly," Taggart glanced around the bar. "Where's Keith tonight?"

Lilly glowered. "That's what I'd like to know. He's been out all day."

Taggart grinned, winding her up. "Maybe he's got a fancy piece, Lilly."

"Hah!" Lilly couldn't take the suggestion seriously. "She'd have to be bloody desperate." She served Taggart with two pints and moved away.

Taggart shifted sideways, closer to his colleague. "So . . . Captain Pugwash has been a naughty boy, has he?"

Livingstone nodded. "Certainly seems so. Maxwell bought the boat direct from Cumbria Cruisers, cash on the nail. Three days later, Samson headed a planning sub-committee which gave Maxwell the exclusive contract to develop the old Eldorado ballroom site."

"Presumably without declaring an interest," Taggart theorised. "Isn't that against some law or other?"

Livingstone smiled. "Yes. It's called bribery and corruption."

Taggart mused for a moment. "I wonder if Kirsty King was part of the deal? A sort of extra sweetener?"

"No," Livingstone seemed very positive. "I got the very strong impression that Maxwell was infatuated with the girl. If anything, he'll have resented Samson for taking her away from him."

Livingstone paused, regarding his superior quietly for a while. "I resent the fact that you didn't try to help me when I was trying to trap Mrs Samson."

Taggart treated the complaint with casual disdain. "Why should I help you? It was your bright idea. You had the Biscuit on your side."

"If she wasn't so attractive . . . would you be so unhelpful?"

Taggart flared, momentarily. "Now don't you *ever* accuse me of that."

Livingstone backed off slightly. "It's just that I think you're sure she did it . . . yet you don't seem too anxious to prove it all of a sudden. Or are you having second thoughts about her guilt?"

Taggart was deliberately noncommittal. "I'm beginning to feel this case has more side issues than we first thought."

"Such as?"

Taggart didn't want to discuss it any more. Not until he had sorted out his own thoughts and theories. "Oh, by the way . . . I have a message for you, from Alison."

"Oh yes?" Livingstone's face brightened up. "What did she say?"

Taggart was straight-faced. "She said thanks, but she's not interested. She prefers her boyfriends to be a bit more exciting."

He watched Livingstone's expression change, saw the hurt in his eyes and felt just a little guilty. "It's nothing personal," he added quickly, to soften the blow somewhat.

It didn't.

Brennan and Petrie sat on a patch of grass, high on a hill above the city. Below them, Glasgow sprawled out into the distance.

"Quite a view," Brennan observed, conversationally.

"I hate it." The youth spat the words out. "Why have you brought me up here?"

"Just to talk," Brennan said. "Just to get to know a few things about you. What does your father do?"

Petrie gave a bitter laugh. "If I knew who the bastard was I might be able to tell you."

"So there's just you and your mother? And you have no job. Things must be hard for you."

"Oh nae," Petrie was sarcastic. "We live in bloody luxury." He was tiring of the pointless conversation. "Look . . . what are you going tae do about these photographs?"

"Keep them. I told you — photography's my hobby." Brennan was silent for a while, savouring the view. He was in a rare, mellow mood, contemplating his new and rosy future. "I might be in a position to offer you a job," he said, finally.

Petrie was suspicious. "What kind of job?"

"My wife and I run a pub," Brennan announced. "Or maybe I should say . . . I run a pub, and my wife runs me."

Petrie smiled thinly. He'd already marked Brennan down as the henpecked type. "I've never done bar work. It's nae my scene."

Brennan turned slightly, to stare the youth straight in the eye. There was a grim smile on his lips. "Oh, it's not bar work, Jimmy."

"What, then?" Petrie had an uneasy feeling.

"I'd like you to kill my wife," Brennan said, as easily as asking the lad to mow his lawn.

Petrie was totally stunned. He stared at Brennan, his eyes wide with disbelief. He would have chosen to treat it as a joke, but the circumstances, and Brennan's cold-blooded attitude, told him it wasn't.

"I'll pay you as well," Brennan went on. "Five thousand pounds . . . in cash. Nice crispy new fivers."

Petrie found his voice at last. "For God's sake! I don't even know your wife."

"Exactly. That's the whole point. You'd have no motive, no connection."

"I don't even know *you*," Petrie added, with heavy emphasis.

Brennan smiled. "Oh but you do, Jimmy. I'm the nice friendly photographer who's going to help you stay out of prison for the next fifteen years." To back up his argument, Brennan slid another couple of stills from his pocket. Petrie stared at them in rising panic. He felt trapped and helpless, like a man having his head held under water.

"How many more of those bloody things have you got?"

"I told you . . . as many as I want," Brennan said. He dropped the threats for a moment and concentrated on the incentives. "Just think what you could do with five thousand pounds, Jimmy. You get away from here . . . this place you hate so much. Go somewhere you could get a job, have a chance, make some sort of future for yourself. There's nothing here for you, Jimmy."

Petrie's voice was choked. "I know that," he hissed. "But murder . . . ?"

Brennan had one last angle of attack. His lips curled into a sneer. "Of course . . . maybe you don't have the bottle to commit a *real* crime. Is that it? Are you a coward, Jimmy?" Brennan stood up and began to walk towards his car.

"Where are you going?" Petrie called after him.

Brennan stopped, turned and smiled. "Home. Give you some time to think about my offer. I'll be in touch . . . soon."

Brennan continued to his car, climbed in and drove off. Petrie remained sitting on the grass, shivering, for a long time. Finally he extracted a crumpled packet of cigarettes from his pocket, stuck one between his lips and lit it with trembling fingers. He stared out over the city, hating it, his life and the cruel trap they had both prepared for him.

Chapter Eight

THEY'D got John Samson out of bed. He opened the door in his dressing gown, yawning, bleary-eyed. He regarded Taggart and Livingstone sleepily for a moment, then consulted his watch. It was just after 8 a.m.

"Do you mind if we come in, Mr Samson?" Taggart asked politely. "We have some more questions we'd like to ask you."

Samson nodded wearily and stepped back, allowing them over the threshold. Closing the front door, he led the way to the breakfast room. He scooped coffee into an electric percolator, filled it and switched it on. "Have you arrested Eleanor yet?" he asked.

"What makes you so sure we're going to?" Taggart countered.

"It's obvious, surely. She was there. She must have waited for me to go before . . ." He tailed off, not wanting to remember the details. "Anyway — ask my father-in-law. She nearly killed him, too," he added, later.

"Do you think he would cover up for her?" Livingstone asked, suddenly.

The question seemed to take Samson aback. He paused for a while, thoughtful. "I don't know," he admitted, finally.

"Where did the boat come from?" Taggart asked.

A flicker of worry crossed Samson's eyes. "Cumbria Cruisers."

Taggart nodded. "Aye . . . we know the manufacturers." He left a long, pregnant pause. "Didn't you recently chair a planning committee which gave Maxwell a development contract worth three-and-a-half million pounds?"

Samson knew that Taggart was on to him. "The boat was a present. You can't prove otherwise."

"A bit of floating nookie worth . . . what, twenty thousand nicker?" Taggart mused.

Samson whirled on him in anger. "Are you always so disrespectful?"

Taggart inclined his head, shaking it. "Oh, I'm being polite, Mr Samson."

"You are aware of the laws governing a councillor's conduct, I suppose?" Livingstone put in.

"Of course," Samson snapped.

"Did you declare your friendship with Maxwell?"

"I can't remember."

Taggart let out a short, explosive laugh. "Aw . . . come on!"

The best form of defence seemed to be in attack. "I thought you were supposed to be investigating Kirsty's murder?"

"Oh, we are," Taggart agreed. "But when you turn over stones, you find all manner of nasty little beasties you didn't expect."

"I don't like your attitude, Detective Inspector."

"Oh!" Taggart digested this information carefully. "Shall I tell you something I don't like, Mr Samson? I've lived in this city all my life. I've seen what's happened to the face of it. Bomb sites where there used to be buildings worth saving. All thanks to people like you." He paused for breath. "Was Kirsty King part of the bribe?"

For a moment, Livingstone thought Samson was going to attack his superior. Then the man slumped his shoulders, glaring at Taggart. "You bastard!"

Taggart let the insult roll off his back. "You didn't answer the question."

The coffee percolator started to bubble. Samson walked across the room to turn it down. "No, she wasn't," he spat back, over his shoulder. "She's dead. My wife killed her. Why the hell don't you go and question *her*?"

"You seem very keen for us to believe that," Taggart observed.

Samson poured himself a cup of black coffee and turned. "You have any better ideas?" He walked back across the kitchen, past the two policemen and into the lounge.

Taggart exchanged a glance and a faint shrug with Livingstone, and followed him. "Did Kirsty King have a sexual relationship with Maxwell before you met her?" he asked, as Samson sat down.

"No!"

The denial was too quick, too emphatic. And Taggart heard the coffee cup rattle in Samson's hand.

"The truth, Mr Samson."

Samson drew in a deep, slow breath. "Yes . . . I think so. But it was all over when we met. Kirsty really cared for me . . . and I for her."

"What about Maxwell?" Livingstone asked. "How did he feel

about it?"

"He wasn't serious about her . . . not like I was," Samson said, and it was obvious that he, at least, believed it. "She was just a young, perhaps impressionable, girl who could be led on." Samson paused, addressing himself to Taggart, "Look — Kirsty was young, she made some mistakes . . . but she wasn't the sort of girl you're trying to make out."

"No . . . perhaps not," Taggart conceded. There was no point in hurting the man any further. He had found out what he needed to know.

Livingstone was admiring Samson's gun cabinet, and its contents. The Purdey was a particularly elegant piece.

"And yes, I do have a licence," Samson said, a trifle bitterly.

"Of course," Livingstone said.

"Start of the season," Taggart observed, for no apparent reason.

The inside of the Petrie's flat reeked of poverty and the despair which attended it. The cheap foam-backed carpet now showed more bare patches than pile. Yellowed, brittle strips of sticky tape made patterns on the cracked windows. Bare light bulbs hung from crumbling, ochre-brown ceilings. The dank, heavy smell of decay hung in the air like a cloud.

Petrie stood in the living room, stripped to the waist, exercising with a chest expander. He found the physical effort helpful in taking his mind off the terrible decision he had to make.

His mother came into the room, a sickly-sweet smile on her lined old face. She was 43, but looked 15 years older. Petrie recognised the smile. It meant she was on the scrounge. "Could you let me have a fiver, son?" Mrs Petrie wheedled. "I'll see you right next week."

Petrie dropped the exerciser, fished in his trouser pocket. He drew out a crumpled note. "This'll leave me skint."

Mrs Petrie took the money anyway. "Next week . . . I promise."

Petrie doubted the promise would be kept. They never were. "You're not behind with the payments again, are ye?"

His mother gave him a beaten, apologetic look. "We can't have them breaking the door down."

Petrie sighed hopelessly. "Aw, Mam . . . when are you ever going to stop paying. It's never ending."

66

"I only have to pay the interest, son . . . don't you worry."

Petrie felt a sudden, burning anger. "You've already paid more than three times what you first borrowed. They'll bleed you dry, those bastards. Why in hell did you go to the moneylenders anyway?"

His mother said nothing. There was nothing to say. He'd know, soon enough. She took a tattered, patched coat off a hook on the back of the door. "I'm just going into town to pick up some more travel brochures. Is there anything you want?"

"Aye. You can get me a packet of cigarettes." Petrie dug deep in his pocket and found another £1 note. He handed it over, and picked up the chest expander again.

"Why do you want muscles, anyway?" his mother asked.

"Tae look good." It was the only answer he could give her.

"Aye," his mother nodded, sighing. She understood. She walked out, closing the door after her.

Petrie heard the front door slam, and threw himself into a spirited regimen of exercise. Finally tired, he moved to the battered old sofa, found a place between the risen springs, and sat down. He reached down over the arm, picking up a handful of colour travel brochures from the hundreds piled there. His mother collected them, week after week. She spent most of her time looking at the pictures of places she would never see, and wouldn't even know where to find on a map. Her answer was always the same when he asked her why she collected them. The sad little smile, and the sad little words: "It's just my wee dream, Jimmy."

Petrie hurled the magazines to the floor again in a furious rage. And the Keith Brennans of the world had five thousand pounds to spend — getting other poor bastards to do their dirty work for them. Petrie felt like crying, although he would never have admitted it to himself.

It looked like a chance meeting — as it was supposed to do. Alison almost bumped into Livingstone in the hospital corridor. She had no way of knowing that he had been pacing that same corridor for twenty minutes, keeping a watchful eye open for a sight of her.

Alison smiled warmly. "Why hello, Peter. If you're here to see Mr Mulholland, you're too late. His daughter collected him first thing this morning."

The news surprised Livingstone. All the same, he found he

couldn't lie about his purpose in the hospital. There was probably no point, anyway. Alison was every bit as sharp as her father.

"No — it was you I came to see," Livingstone said.

"Me? Why?" Alison looked surprised.

"To confront you face to face," Livingstone said. He felt himself begin to flush, and wished he hadn't forced the confrontation after all.

Alison looked baffled now. "Confront me? About what, Peter?"

Livingstone bristled with righteous indignation. "I think you've got a bloody cheek," he said. "Not only do you lead me on . . . you have the insensitivity to send a message like that with your father . . . when you know full well how things are between us."

Alison was beginning to doubt for his sanity. "Peter . . . I have not the faintest idea what you're talking about. What message?"

Livingstone fell silent, feeling awkward and confused. Dim and distant bells were beginning to ring in the back of his mind. "Thanks, but you're not interested? You didn't say that?"

"To whom?"

"To your father."

Alison shook her head. "All I told my father was that we were going out together on Saturday night. We *are*, aren't we?"

"Damn right we are," Livingstone said firmly. "I'll pick you up at eight. At home."

Jaw clenched, he strode off down the corridor, seething with anger.

Mulholland sat back in his favourite easy chair, resting. Eleanor busied herself tidying up for him, avoiding any real contact. They made polite conversation, but it was forced, unnatural. There was a barrier between them. It had been there from the first moment she had shown up at the hospital to collect him.

"You'll have to get a housekeeper — a nice young one," Eleanor said.

"No excitement, remember?" There was no humour in the old man's voice. "Are you still staying with Donald?"

"Yes. He's very good to me."

Mulholland grunted. "You were always close to him."

The comment seemed to call for some response. Eleanor crossed the room and sat down on the arm of her father's chair.

"Unlike us," she murmured, sadly. Mulholland made no reply. "I *was* with her," Eleanor said after a while. "But I didn't kill her."

There was a long silence. Mulholland didn't even seem to have heard her. "She was a sweet girl," he murmured, distantly, at last. "John was a lucky man."

Eleanor jumped from the chair as though she had been scalded. "John . . . John. You always sided with him. Did it never occur to you to think of my feelings."

"He was a good husband to you," Mulholland said. It was as if they were trying to conduct a conversation through an interpreter who had already left the room. The standard excuses, accusations and counter-accusations came trotting out, as they always did.

"I had my career."

"And you put it before everybody. John, Graeme, your mother. The night she died you couldn't even be there because you had a performance."

"And where were you when she was alive? With other women, most of the time."

"At least I was with her when she died. I held her hand, and explained as best I could that you were too busy to come and see her."

They both fell silent, smarting from each other's familiar taunts and old guilts. There was no point in even attempting apologies or reconciliations.

In the absence of Livingstone, Taggart had asked McVitie into the interview room for Maxwell's questioning. The builder's resentment at being dragged away from his work showed in his defiant, mocking attitude. He was, Taggart had decided, a man who considered himself above the law.

Confronted with the facts about the boat, Maxwell seemed unconcerned. He gave Taggart a condescending smile. "Graft goes on all the time . . . and you know it."

"Bribing a councillor is against the law," McVitie put in, rather superfluously.

Maxwell laughed openly. "Enough of you boys are open to it."

Taggart leapt from his seat and threw himself across the desk in one movement. He stabbed his forefinger towards Maxwell's face, inches from his eyes. He was blazing. "Oh . . . you just try it, son, and see where it gets you."

"Easy, Jim," McVitie placed a restraining hand on his arm, easing him back into his chair.

Taggart settled down, swallowing his anger. With some satisfaction, he noted that the grin had been wiped off Maxwell's face. Yet he was still defiant.

"Where do you think Mulholland's money came from? Back in the Sixties he was buying his worst enemies to carve this city up."

"How long did Kirsty King work for you?" McVitie asked.

"Eight months."

"Was she your mistress?" Taggart watched the man's face as he asked the question. It was sullen, noncommital.

"That's my business."

Was he just being uncooperative or trying to protect the girl's reputation? Taggart wasn't sure. "She was murdered. That makes it our business."

"All right. I slept with her occasionally. Do you want dates? Details?"

"Don't try to be clever, Mr Maxwell," Taggart cautioned. "Was she part and parcel of the bribe to sweeten Samson?"

Maxwell looked genuinely shocked at the suggestion, Taggart noticed.

"No, of course not."

"Perhaps she wasn't supposed to desert you for Samson . . . or not entirely. Is that it?"

Maxwell evaded the question completely. "I didn't kill her," he said quietly.

It seemed an odd thing to say, at that particular point. McVitie and Taggart exchanged a quizzical look.

"Who suggested you did?" McVitie asked.

"I was in my office. All that day. My new secretary will vouch for that," Maxwell went on.

"I've no doubt," Taggart muttered. He was wondering why the man had so suddenly become defensive. He needed time to think about it. He pushed back his chair, standing. "You can go now. You'll be hearing from us."

Maxwell seemed surprised at the abrupt end to the interview. He stood up and walked to the door. By the time he reached it, he had thought of a parting shot. "You think you're all so pure, don't you?" he sneered, before making his exit.

Taggart looked across at McVitie, who raised his eyebrows.

"Strange," McVitie said.

Taggart nodded. "For all his bluster . . . I get the feeling he's scared of something."

"Or someone," McVitie added.

It was food for thought. Taggart pondered on it on the way back to his office.

Livingstone was waiting for him. "I've just been to the hospital," he said, heavily.

Taggart faked a solicitous smile. "Nothing terminal, I hope?"

"Alison said she gave you no such message."

Taggart looked contrite. "Sorry . . . I must have got it mixed up."

Livingstone gave up the idea of shaming him into an apology. "I'm taking her out on Saturday night," he announced.

Taggart nodded absently. "Yes . . . you do that, Peter." He turned away, so that Livingstone couldn't see the grin on his face.

Chapter Nine

ANOTHER day, Taggart thought, waking up in the armchair in the lounge once again. Another day to be spent turning over stones, watching the maggots and the crawling things face the light of exposure. And another day in which a young girl's murder went unsolved.

He dragged himself up the stairs, avoiding the creaky patch on the top step. Jean was still asleep, in the double bed which he was still free to share and now rarely did. Alison was gone, on early shift. Taggart wondered, briefly, if she ever felt as hopeless as he did. Her job, after all, was every bit as depressing as his. Sudden death and suffering were major factors in her day to day existence. But then she always had the hope of cure, recovery. At the very best, Taggart's answer to death was merely retribution.

He ran a bath and immersed himself, trying to soak away the troubles of a day yet to come. That was the worst part — knowing that it could never change, never get any better. People would always lie, cheat, steal . . . kill. And he would always be there just one step behind.

He shaved in the bath. It was a lazy habit, and one which always made him feel slightly guilty. Afterwards, he regretted it. More weight to carry through the day.

The Press were already gathered around the entrance to the rehearsal hall when Taggart arrived. Like vultures, he thought. He kept his distance, also waiting, uncomfortably aware that he wasn't so different.

Eleanor Samson arrived at 8.30 a.m., a full hour before rehearsals were due to start. She had hoped to avoid her reception committee, and was disappointed that she had failed. She braced herself, and marched towards them.

She seemed almost relieved as Taggart slipped into step beside her. At least he was an irritation she was getting used to, learning how to handle. "Early bird," Eleanor said. She nodded towards the small crowd of reporters and photographers. "And another whole flock of them. Why do I feel like the worm?"

Taggart took her arm as the Press descended on them with a barrage of questions and exploding flashguns. He steered her through the door. The hall was empty. Eleanor sighed and drew a deep breath as Taggart shooed away the most persistent reporter and closed the door.

"According to them I've already been tried and found guilty," Eleanor said.

Taggart suddenly felt sorry for her, and said so.

Eleanor regarded him quizzically for a second, seeing a side of him which she had not even suspected existed. She managed a faint smile. "I'm not blaming you," she said quietly.

They walked across the hall towards the stage, their footsteps echoing hollowly.

"There are two kinds of life sentence, Mrs Samson," Taggart observed, philosophically. "The kind you serve in prison. The kind you serve out."

Eleanor looked at him strangely, unable to fathom his mood.

"There are people free today who are guilty of murder," Taggart went on. "All we lack is proof. All they lack is the hope that we'll ever give up and that one day they'll be forgotten about."

"I've never known freedom," Eleanor said. "So your little homily is wasted."

"Never?" Taggart asked, surprised.

"All I have is a professional life. I suppose it's much the same for you."

Taggart shrugged, "I have a family life. I try to hold on to that."

Eleanor regarded him enviously. "I had that. I threw it away."

"You really wanted him back?" Taggart asked, curious.

Eleanor nodded. "For six years."

"How badly, Mrs Samson? How far were you prepared to go?"

Eleanor sat down on the edge of the stage. She looked up at Taggart with wide-open eyes. "Are you still convinced I killed her?"

"I was never *convinced*," Taggart told her. "Did you?"

Eleanor managed a smile. "I suppose this is what's called the psychological approach. The 'nice' policeman."

"I don't have to be." It was a flat statement, not a threat.

Eleanor was about to answer him when the rehearsal room door opened unexpectedly. "Molly!" Eleanor reacted to the woman who entered with affection. She stood, ran across to meet her and embraced her warmly.

Taggart stood, regarding them with morose resignation. For a moment he had thought he was getting somewhere.

"This is Detective Chief Inspector Taggart," Eleanor said. "Molly Baron, my agent." She turned back to Molly, the introductions completed. "I didn't expect to see you."

"I wasn't going to let you struggle through this on your own." The woman turned on Taggart, assertively. "Is this an official visit? If so, aren't you policemen supposed to work in pairs?"

"Like oxen, you mean?" Taggart cracked, failing to raise a smile.

"I do know something about procedure," Molly said coldly.

Taggart took the hint. "I was just leaving." He turned to Eleanor, briefly. "Still that unanswered question, Mrs Samson."

She made no reply as he walked out.

Taggart returned to the office to learn that Livingstone had left with McVitie to interview Mulholland once again. It was a mixed blessing. On the one hand it gave him some free time to sort out his own thoughts, on the other it increased his sense of vexation. He really was beginning to resent the personal interest McVitie was taking in the case. The Super could assure him that he wasn't watching Taggart's back as many times as he liked. It still didn't make the story convincing.

It was also, Taggart was convinced, a waste of police time. He was sure that Mulholland had nothing more to contribute. Further, he was even beginning to think that no one they had spoken to so far had much more to offer — even Eleanor. Short of a direct confession, she now showed every indication of remaining a dead end. There were new avenues of exploration, somewhere. The trouble was, they'd neglected to give him a map.

Two hours of uninterrupted thought brought nothing, except that the early morning depression gave way to mid-morning blues. When Livingstone phoned in to announce he was having lunch with McVitie, Taggart was feeling practically paranoic. He knew the symptoms . . . and the cure. By noon, he was ensconced at the bar of the Firhill Tavern, draining his second large scotch.

Lilly sidled up the bar to serve him. "Another?"

"Aye," Taggart grunted.

"Don't see you on your own very much these days," Lilly said, chattily. "Where's the young one with the posh voice today?"

"Hob-nobbing with the high and mighty," Taggart said. He paid for the drink and moved away from the bar to pre-empt any further conversation.

"Morning, Mr Taggart."

Taggart sighed, turning to face Brennan, who had just come in to the bar from upstairs. "Morning, Keith." He hoped that would be enough. It wasn't. Brennan seemed unusually cheery and self-confident.

"Have you arrested anyone for the boat murder yet?"

"Not yet." Taggart wished he would go away.

"Any ideas?"

"A few." Taggart was deliberately terse, hoping that Brennan would get the message, but it seemed he was just warming to his subject.

"What a name, eh? Kirsty King. Sounds like something out of *Dallas*."

"That's probably where she got it from," Taggart said wearily. He prepared himself for the next banal comment, but it never came.

Brennan suddenly shot away with a vague wave of his hand. Taggart sought not to question the fates which so unexpectedly rescued him. It was time to make his escape. He drained the Scotch glass and headed for the door, brushing past a scruffily-dressed youth who had just walked in.

Petrie looked around for a second or two before walking to the bar. He glanced at Brennan, who returned the look without recognition.

Lilly moved to serve him.

"Pint of heavy," Petrie stared at her piercingly as she poured the beer.

It was a look impossible to ignore. Lilly caught his eyes. Cold. Reptilian. On drugs, she told herself. Sniffing glue, or something like that. It couldn't be anything personal, him staring at her like that. She didn't know him. There was no connection between them.

Samson was waiting outside the house as Maxwell drove up. Maxwell climbed out of the car.

"What do you want to talk to me about?" He saw the anger on Samson's face and knew the answer.

"Well — how did the police find out about the boat?" Samson demanded.

"I left the brochure on my desk. This bright young spark noticed it and put two and two together."

"How much did you tell them?" Samson wanted to know.

"Not much. I admitted nothing. Just told them a few of the facts of life, that's all."

Samson groaned, "That was stupid."

"Don't worry about it," Maxwell tried to reassure him. "We broke the First Commandment, that's all. Thou shalt not get caught." He paused, looking more serious. "OK. I'm sorry I dropped you in it. I lost my rattle."

Samson looked despondent. "You've probably lost me a damned sight more." He was silent for some time. When he spoke again, his voice was calm, but threatening. "If there *is* an official enquiry . . . I'm not taking the can on my own, you realise that?"

"It won't come to that."

"It had better not, Ted. I warn you now . . . if I go down, I'm taking you with me. I've got names, dates, amounts paid. I'll use them all if I have to. Anything which will keep me out of the slammer."

"You bastard! You would, too. You took the bribes . . . you were supposed to take the risks as well."

Samson opened his mouth to fire back, but changed his mind. From the corner of his eye he had seen Graeme walking up the drive, home from school. "We'll talk about this another time," he hissed to Maxwell. "Play it cool for now, eh?"

They both fell silent as Graeme approached.

"Afternoon, Graeme. How's school?" Maxwell made the effort to seem friendly. It was not returned.

"Fine," Graeme said curtly. He merely nodded at his father, and walked into the house.

"Don't teach them conversation, do they?" Maxwell said. Without a word of goodbye to Samson, he turned, got into his car and drove off.

Samson looked after the departing car, a frown creasing his forehead. He was wondering if it had been a wise thing to threaten the man so directly. Ted Maxwell had come up the hard way.

Word had it he was a dangerous man to cross.

He had other things to worry about. Graeme was obviously in one of his awkward moods. Samson pushed Ted Maxwell from his mind and went into the house after his son.

Graeme had taken off his blazer and was sitting on the bed. The door was open, but Samson tapped on it anyway. "Can I come in?" he enquired cheerily.

Graeme looked up morosely. "Of course."

"Well, am I going to see much of you this weekend?" Samson asked, to get some sort of conversation going.

Graeme shrugged. "That's up to you. I've got a match tomorrow. You can come and see me play if you like."

Samson forced some enthusiasm. "Yes, I'd like that." Silence fell for a while. "Would you like a beer?" Samson offered.

"No thanks." The boy shook his head.

Silence again. It was hard work, but Samson persevered. "You know — you never sit down with me and have a beer. Now I'll bet if your mother offered you one . . ."

"Yes, well she wouldn't, would she?" In six years, Samson had forgotten that Eleanor was teetotal.

Samson sighed, admitting defeat. The friendly father approach obviously wasn't going to work. Perhaps Graeme was still upset about Kirsty's death. Perhaps he would welcome the chance to talk seriously instead of attempting bantering conversation. "Look, Graeme. Perhaps you never approved of Kirsty, but she was a smashing girl. She meant a lot to me, you know."

"I know that."

"She liked you," Samson said. "Even though you never made the effort to like her." He paused, choosing his words carefully. "It's not as though she came along to smash up my marriage to your mother or anything like that. Your mother and I would never have got back together, you must realise that."

"Why not? She was willing to try." Emotion choked Graeme's voice.

Sadly, Samson realised that his son remained fiercely loyal to Eleanor, and would never understand his point of view. "You care about your mother more than anybody, don't you? Even after what she did to you."

"She did nothing to me," Graeme's voice blazed with sudden anger.

"She walked out on you," Samson reminded him. "She chose to be famous instead of be a mother."

It was a truth Graeme had refused to accept for most of his life. He still would not face it. "Stop trying to turn me against her. You've always tried to do that."

Samson found himself on the defensive. "That's not true and not fair. I've tried to be a father to you — give you some masculine influence. It's not healthy, this obsession of yours with your mother. You never bring girls home, when your mother is away you spend all your spare time writing to her."

"I like writing," Graeme said sullenly. The hidden implications in his father's words suddenly struck him. "You think I'm gay? Is that it?"

It wasn't what Samson had meant. Nevertheless, the possibility had been raised now. It hung in the air between them. Samson said nothing.

Perhaps Graeme had expected, even needed, a denial. The silence was like an accusation. Tears welled in his eyes. Anger and resentment erupted inside him like liquid fire. "I could prove there was nothing wrong with me. I could . . . if I wanted to." Graeme screamed the words, almost hysterically. Then he jumped from the bed and ran from the room, sobbing.

Petrie waited on the street corner, impatient, nervous. Taking a last draw on a cigarette, he dropped it to join the stubs of three others and ground it underfoot. He paced up and down a few times, looking up the street for Brennan's car.

Brennan came from the other direction, pulling up behind the youth. Petrie started, caught unawares. He was very jittery.

"Been waiting long?" Brennan asked.

Petrie shrugged, affecting bravado. "Nae. Not long," he lied.

"Well?" Brennan said.

"In the pub . . . was that her?"

Brennan nodded gravely. "Aye, that was her."

Lilly's face was still etched into Petrie's mind. "Why do you want to kill her?" The question was a plea.

"I have my reasons." Brennan didn't want to go into details for the moment. "Have you considered my offer?"

"Aye," Petrie's voice dropped to a whisper. "I'll do it. I haven't got much choice, have I?"

Brennan repressed a smile of triumph. He leaned over and opened the passenger door. "Get in," he said. "We have some plans to make."

Chapter Ten

IT was the second day running that McVitie had taken Livingstone under his wing, and the young man felt slightly guilty about it. Not that he would have admitted any loyalty to Taggart, especially since the unpleasant business over Alison. Nevertheless, he had misgivings, and felt it only right to voice them.

McVitie had just pulled up outside Don Mulholland's house — the address Eleanor Samson had given them. "If you don't mind me saying so, sir . . . I do feel that Detective Chief Inspector Taggart should have been told what we are doing. I wouldn't like him to feel that I was working behind his back, so to speak."

McVitie dismissed the objection. "Does Jim always tell you what he's doing?" he countered.

Livingstone fell silent. The Superintendent had a point.

They sat watching the front of the house for a while. McVitie seemed in no great hurry to get to work. "Do you still have family in Edinburgh?" he asked conversationally.

"My parents and two brothers," Livingstone answered.

"Either of your brothers thinking of following your footsteps?"

"I doubt it," Livingstone said. He did not elaborate.

"Pity," McVitie said. "We need more bright young men in the force."

Livingstone accepted the implied compliment without comment. McVitie seemed to be hedging round something, and Livingstone felt awkward about it. "Matthew Kerr's Academy, weren't you?" McVitie went on.

"That's right, sir."

"Play rugby, did you?"

"Not a great deal. I preferred tennis."

"Ah!" McVitie nodded. He seemed a little disappointed. "I was rugby captain there, you know. 1944," he volunteered.

Livingstone was surprised. "Really, sir? I didn't know."

McVitie smiled. "That I was an old boy . . . or I played rugby?" He paused for a second, his smile becoming almost crafty. "By the way . . . I wouldn't mention it to Jim, if I were you. Don't want him getting paranoid, do we?"

Livingstone was expected to share the secret joke. He made an effort. "The Old Boy network, sir?"

"And the rugby," McVitie said. "Jim doesn't much care for that, either."

Strangely enough, Taggart was, at that very moment, watching a rugby match. Or, more accurately, he was watching one of the players taking part in a rugby match. He had studied Graeme's style of play carefully, wondering if it came out in his personal life. On the field, the boy was aggressive, impulsive, charging in where others might fear physical injury. A team player . . . but an individualist as well. A boy with conflicting loyalties.

Samson felt like a criminal, a sneak-thief. He had never invaded his son's privacy before and he hated doing it now. It was ultimately for the boy's own good, he kept telling himself. Something had recently gone very wrong with their relationship, and it needed to be put right. Even on the brink of manhood, Samson felt sure that a son needed a close bond to his father — a mutual trust and understanding.

That was Samson's justification. He repressed the nagging, persistent little voice which told him his actions were purely for his own peace of mind. The conversation the previous afternoon had upset Samson deeply, infringing as it had done upon a personally strong and deep loathing. But the issue of his son's sexuality, his manhood, had been brought into question, and Samson had to have an answer.

He probed carefully in Graeme's chest of drawers, lifting neat piles of socks and underclothes so as not to disturb them. There was nothing. Samson went through the wardrobe and through the box in which Graeme kept his sports equipment. Other than a few postcards from Eleanor in exotic places, there was nothing there either.

Samson was about to leave Graeme's bedroom when memory of his own youth turned him back. He walked back to the bed, lifting the mattress, recalling where he had always hidden his most secret things. He smiled as he came across a pile of magazines and letters. So nothing much had changed in 26 years. Perhaps he and his son were not so alienated as he had feared. He sat down on the edge of the bed to check through the cache.

There were a couple of copies of *Playboy* magazine and some Swedish hard-core porn books. Samson grinned to himself, almost with relief. He wasn't a prude. In his day it had been simpler and less graphic pin-up material, but the principle remained the same. His son showed a normal and natural appetite for the opposite sex.

Samson flipped through the letters idly, not wanting to read them in any detail. He had found out what he wanted to know, and any further intrusion would only increase his sense of guilt. The stiff-backed exercise book was different, however. A casual glance was enough to tell Samson that it was a diary. He had not been aware that Graeme kept a record of his life and thoughts, but now he was aware of it, he realised that it might also hold the clue to his recent behaviour.

Samson flipped through to the most recent entries and started to read them. Almost at once, the smile on his face started to fade. By the time he had backtracked to the entries for the previous month, Samson's face was ashen. His hands were trembling. He felt a strange tightness in his throat. He could feel his heart pounding, pumping adrenalin-enriched blood through his system. The flight or fight syndrome. Both primitive emotional responses tore at Samson's self-control.

Eventually he could take no more. He stood, shakily, dropping the diary on to the bed. Like a man in a trance, he headed for the door, hardly seeing it through a mist of tears.

Moments later, Samson climbed into his Range Rover and started it up. In Graeme's bedroom, the diary lay open at the last entry Samson had read. The record, dated one month previously, of Graeme's first sexual encounter with Kirsty King.

Bored, Taggart consulted his watch. There were just over fifteen minutes of the match left. He forced his attention back to the rugby field, not really taking any interest in the game. He'd stuck it out so far, he might as well hang around. And he did want to talk to Graeme.

Taggart was unaware of Samson's Range Rover until it pulled into his field of vision, bumping over the grass parallel to the actual pitch. Several spectators hastily moved out of the way as the speeding vehicle headed straight for them and finally skidded to a halt.

Taggart watched, fascinated, as Samson stepped out of the vehicle and left the door open and the engine running. He walked straight on to the pitch, moving like an automaton.

The game faltered and stopped as the players saw him coming. The referee broke into a run, whistle shrilling, waving his hands to order the intruder off the playing area. Samson was oblivious to it all. He continued marching in a dead straight line, seeing nothing except a dancing red haze in which the solitary figure of his son stood out in sharp focus.

Graeme moved away from the other players, as if to greet his father. The look of surprise on his face changed to one of hopelessness as Samson closed the last few yards which separated them. His father's face was like a death mask. With chilling certainty, Graeme knew that his father had discovered his betrayal. Rising above his fear, there was a sense of ultimate relief. He had carried the terrible guilt for too long. Knowing what was about to happen, Graeme stood his ground. In other circumstances Samson would have been proud of him.

Father and son stood stock still, face to face. There were no words to say. Finally, Samson swung his body like a golfer, twisting at the waist and pivoting on the balls of his feet. He whipped back, savagely and violently, throwing every muscle in his body into the back-handed slap aimed at Graeme's face. The blow knocked the boy sideways, stunned. He lay sprawled out on the grass, looking mutely up at his father through tear-filled eyes.

The drama seemed to have been enacted in slow-motion, freezing into a tableau. Now the action came to life as the players reacted.

Three of the larger youths threw themselves on Samson, trying to pinion his arms and drag him to the ground. Samson struggled violently, lashing out in all directions with his feet. The referee tried desperately to fight his way into the mêlée, with little success. Mob violence took root and spread, as other players from both sides found themselves irresistibly drawn into the fray.

Taggart loped across the field, drawing his ID card from his pocket on the way. Reaching the struggling mass, he went for the referee first, grabbing his arm and pulling him clear. "It's a family affair," Taggart shouted, waving his ID in totally random fashion. "Break it up now . . . Police."

The scuffling ceased abruptly. The players backed off, keeping their distance. Samson stared at Taggart blankly for a moment, then turned and walked away without a word.

Taggart bent over Graeme, offering a hand. The boy took it, allowing Taggart to pull him to his feet. Their eyes met, and a family secret was shared. It was not the time to discuss it. Taggart's face cracked into a lopsided grin. "Never did understand the rules of this game," he said.

Through his pain, Graeme managed a weak smile. He felt as though a great burden had been lifted from him. He had needed a man to talk to, to understand, for so long.

Graeme was silent on the drive home. Taggart didn't push the boy, respecting his need to get his jangled thoughts together. Samson was in the front garden as they drove up to the house. He busied himself in some heavy digging, ignoring them. Taggart said nothing, understanding. Hard physical labour was as good a way as any to release the kind of seething internal emotions the man must be feeling. He followed Graeme into the house and into his bedroom.

The diary still lay on the bed. Taggart picked it up, glanced at the open pages.

"It's private," Graeme said, uncertainly.

Taggart nodded. He tossed the exercise book to the very end of the bed. "You should never write down what you don't want people to read," he observed. He paused, looking at Graeme, wondering if he was ready. "Do you want to talk about it?" he prompted, eventually.

Graeme nodded wordlessly.

"Who started it?" Taggart asked, gently.

"She did. Dad left her at home one morning. I was supposed to be doing some homework."

"And?"

Graeme's face registered disgust at the memory. "It was horrible. She asked me, right out . . . would you like to . . ." He didn't finish the sentence.

"Was she your first?" Taggart was on delicate ground, and he knew it. The first wrong word, the merest hint of ridicule, and the boy would close up like a clam.

"Yes," Graeme admitted, a trifle sheepishly.

"Did she know that?"

"Yes," Graeme whispered. "She thought it was funny," he added, bitterly.

"And you felt guilty afterwards?"

"Of course."

"Then why did you do it?" Taggart asked, realising the question was stupid as he mouthed the words. He smiled, continuing quickly. "Daft question . . . eh?" He flashed Graeme a man-to-man look, which seemed to help the boy. He gave Taggart a nervous smile.

"How many times did it happen afterwards?"

Graeme shrugged. "Five or six . . . I'm not sure."

"And did you feel jealous of your father?"

"No." The answer was quick and emphatic.

"I want the truth, Graeme," Taggart said.

"That is the truth." Taggart accepted it.

"How did you feel about him going off with her for two weeks, eh?"

Graeme gave a nervous laugh. "I was pleased. Can you understand that?"

Taggart said nothing, encouraging Graeme to elaborate.

"I felt scared . . . about Dad finding out. I felt guilty, knowing how he felt about her. I was confused . . . I just wanted her to go away."

"She did, Graeme," Taggart muttered quietly. He was silent for some while, studying Graeme's face. "Is there anything else you want to tell me?" he asked, finally.

Graeme looked puzzled. "What else could there be?"

Taggart let it ride for a while, giving Graeme a chance to have second thoughts, volunteer any more information. Nothing came. Taggart hadn't really expected anything. Things were rarely that simple.

Taggart stood up. "I have to go now, Graeme. Will you be all right?"

Graeme nodded wordlessly. He stared out of his bedroom window as Taggart left.

Samson saw Taggart coming out of the house and thrust the spade viciously into the soil one last time. He straightened, wiping his hands on the back of his trousers.

Taggart walked right up to him. "Remember, he's only eighteen," he muttered.

Samson said nothing. His face was set, impassive. He turned away and marched towards the house.

Taggart sucked at his lip, shrugging. It was a domestic quarrel. There was nothing more he could say or do.

Chapter Eleven

PETRIE was nervous. "Why did we have to meet here?" he demanded peevishly. He and Brennan were in Calderpark Zoo, walking towards the lion enclosure.

Brennan was surprised. "Don't you like zoos?"

Petrie shuddered with distaste. "I hate them. I hate to see animals all locked up like that . . . in cages. Trapped. Like me."

"Very educational, zoos," Brennan observed philosophically. "We can learn a lot from animals." He broke off, pointing at a lioness tearing a piece of raw meat. "See . . . animals kill without a second thought. Without compunction."

"We're nae animals."

Brennan smiled distantly. "Oh yes we are, Jimmy. A higher species, that's all."

Petrie was silent for a while, thinking. The one question Brennan had refused to answer was still on his mind. "Why do you want to kill her, anyway?"

Brennan stared thoughtfully at the youth before answering. There seemed no good reason not to tell him, at this late stage. "Because she's *my* cage, Jimmy. She owns the Firhill and she won't sell it. With the money I can make from the sale of the site, I can get away from here."

Petrie looked crafty, suddenly. "You'll be making a lot more than five thousand pounds, then?"

Brennan read the youth like a badly-written book. "Yes . . . but *you* won't," he said pointedly. "I still have the photographs, remember?"

Petrie fell silent, sulking. Vague dreams of blackmail died as quickly as they had been born.

"It will have to be done at exactly four o'clock," Brennan was saying. "Lilly always takes an afternoon nap between three and five. Never fails. It'll have to look like a break-in which went wrong. A casual thief, caught in the act and panicking. Nothing premeditated."

"Supposing someone sees me?"

"Nobody will see you," Brennan assured him. "The land's derelict at the back. There's a side door. I'll make sure it's unlocked. There's stairs that go up to the flat. The bar will be closed at that time. Lilly never did approve of all-day opening."

"If it's all that easy . . . why don't you do it yourself?" Petrie wanted to know.

Brennan sighed with exasperation. Sometimes Petrie's stupidity annoyed him. "Because I'd be the first person the police would suspect. The husband always is. This way, I can be establishing an unbreakable alibi."

Brennan suddenly grinned like a schoolboy. It was as if by just talking about it, the affair was over and done. "Come on . . . let's go and see the monkeys."

Lilly woke with a start, and threw her legs over the side of the day-bed. She winced with agony, suddenly remembering why she had slept later than usual. She glanced at her watch. It was 5.30 p.m.

She stood, rubbing her legs to ease the pain away. It didn't work. Stretching, she hobbled towards the stair and down into the bar.

Olive regarded her sympathetically as she limped in. "Your legs still playing you up, love?"

"Aye. They're no better, I'm afraid. Thanks for helping out, Olive. You opened up okay, then?"

Olive smiled cheerily. "No trouble at all, Lilly. I'm sure I can manage on my own until Keith gets back. You go and have some more rest. It's the best thing. My Jack suffered for years with varicose veins, so I know what it's like, dear. Go on . . . go back and lie down."

"You die lying down," Lilly said, but the idea was tempting. She looked round the bar. Only two customers. She nodded at Olive. "Perhaps you're right. Just for another hour or so." She hobbled back to the flat, laying it on a bit for Olive's benefit.

One of the two customers was Taggart. He was sitting at a table with his back to the bar. He'd been outside the front door when Olive unbolted it. He sipped his drink quietly for a few minutes, going over the events of the day in his head.

The door opened. Livingstone came in, saw Taggart and walked towards him.

"Slumming?" Taggart asked.

"Desk Sergeant said you were here." Livingstone crossed to the bar, ordered a pint and returned to the table. He sat down.

"Have a good day?" Taggart asked.

Livingstone studied Taggart's face for a trace of sarcasm, failing to find it. "No, not really," he admitted. He was silent for a while, framing his words. "I suppose you know that McVitie wanted me to go with him to interview Eleanor Samson again?"

"Aye." Taggart appeared unconcerned.

"Just for the record, I did make the point that it might be out of order."

Taggart accepted this information stoically. He affected a faint shrug. "The Biscuit has the rank. He makes the orders."

"Just thought you ought to know, that's all."

"So how did it go?"

Livingstone took a long drink and put the glass down on the table. "Not terribly well. She still sticks to her story."

Taggart gave a little shake of his head. "Brave lady, that."

Livingstone looked surprised. "Brave?"

"You don't know women," Taggart told him. "Maybe you should learn a bit more about them before you take Alison out."

Livingstone let the little dig go. He'd walked into it. He fell silent again for a while, thinking.

"So?" Taggart asked. He could tell the young man had something on his mind.

"McVitie's asked me to prepare a report. For the Procurator Fiscal," Livingstone blurted out.

Taggart's mouth dropped open. "What?"

Livingstone shrugged, as if to express his agreement with Taggart's surprise. "He thinks there might be enough circumstantial evidence on which to charge her."

It was the last straw. Taggart fought to control his anger and failed. He drained his drink and slammed it down on the table. "Right," he said, explosively, rising from his chair. He stormed out of the pub, nearly knocking Brennan over as he came in through the door.

McVitie was just about to get into his car as Taggart stomped into the station forecourt. He saw the black look on Taggart's face and prepared himself for trouble.

"I'm acting in perfect accordance with procedure, Jim," McVitie said, knowing full well what Taggart was so annoyed about. "I think we may have just enough to start preparing a case."

"You said yourself we have no forensic evidence of any value." Taggart didn't understand his superior's seemingly sudden hurry to bring the case to court.

"We have three interviews, a few little slips she nearly made today. We have motive, opportunity, and a reputable eye-witness. She's already lost most of her bluster. I think that in a court of law she might just crack."

"I've not even seen a report of the last interview," Taggart pointed out.

"There's a full transcript waiting on your desk." McVitie had covered himself on that particular socre.

Taggart felt his frustrations bubbling up. This verbal fencing was not getting things out into the open, as he had intended. He jumped, abruptly, to the crux of the matter. "We're not getting to the point, are we, sir? What I really object to is that you saw fit to go over my head and ask that . . ."

McVitie didn't give him a chance to finish. Now he was angry, and he let it show. "That *what?* He's your neighbour, Jim. He knows what it's about. And he isn't susceptible to Eleanor Samson's charms."

"Meaning you think I am?"

"She's a beautiful woman. She's successful, and famous. But we can't let it be seen that there is one law for her and one for the rest of us."

Suddenly Taggart understood McVitie's hurry to finish the case. Those words — 'can't let it be seen' — gave it all away. "So that's what it's all about. We're getting some bad Press. Trial by journalist now, is it?"

McVitie looked slightly sheepish. "There have been certain . . . suggestions in the media, yes," he admitted. "Kirsty King was a very young and very attractive girl. She makes a sympathetic victim and good copy."

"Let me tell you something about this 'sympathetic victim' of yours," Taggart fired back. "She seduced Samson's son. So far we know that she bedded Maxwell, Samson and Graeme . . . all in the course of the last couple of months. It would seem our innocent little victim isn't quite what she first appeared to be."

McVitie was somewhat taken aback by these latest revelations. "How did you find this out?"

"In the course of doing my job." The sarcasm in Taggart's voice was plain, and quite deliberate.

McVitie reflected for a while. "Does Peter know about this?"

"Not unless he's clairvoyant. He's been rather busy doing other things recently."

It was time for McVitie to reassert his authority. He glared angrily, his voice becoming threatening. " Don't start knocking the system, Jim. You two start working against each other, and . . ."

"Start?" Taggart interrupted. He turned away in disgust and walked towards the station.

McVitie opened his mouth to call after him, then changed his mind. He climbed into his car and drove off.

"Where's Peter?" Alison asked as soon as Taggart walked into the house. It was not the sort of greeting he needed, under the circumstances.

His reply was untypically sharp. "Isn't he capable of making his own arrangements?"

Alison looked hurt. "I just thought he might have come home with you, that's all."

Taggart felt lousy. He softened. "Well he didn't. I'm sorry. It didn't occur to me to suggest it."

The apology seemed to work. Alison nodded understandingly. "Hard day?"

Taggart forced a smile. "Not one of the best." He threw his coat on to the hallstand and walked towards the lounge.

Jean was reading the evening paper. She looked up as Taggart came in. "It says here that Eleanor Samson was questioned by the police again today. You?"

Taggart shook his head. "McVitie . . . and the boy wonder."

"Her new tour is due to start in a few weeks. It's rumoured she might not even sing."

"She'll sing," Taggart said confidently. "She's a fighter, that one." He stepped over to Jean and kissed her on the forehead. "Like you."

A car horn tooted twice outside the house. Taggart crossed to the window, recognising Livingstone's car. "Hello . . . Young Casanova's here."

Jean flashed him a warning look "There's not going to be an

argument about Alison going out, is there?"

Taggart feigned injured innocence. "An argument? Me? Why should there be?"

Even Alison looked at him suspiciously. "Do you mean that, Dad?"

"Of course. I want you to go out with Peter. I think it might help his problem. You see, he's never been very successful with girls."

Alison chose to ignore the snide remark. "I like him, that's all. Thanks, Dad." She kissed Taggart on the cheek, and hurried out to meet Livingstone.

Taggart watched from the window as she danced down the short drive and climbed into the car. Livingstone drove off immediately. Taggart turned back into the room, a strange smile on his face.

"What are you plotting?" Jean asked.

"Plotting? Me?" Again, Taggart looked as though butter wouldn't melt in his mouth.

"I know that look, Jim Taggart," his wife said, and left it at that.

Chapter Twelve

ONE and a half days without police harassment was like a holiday, Eleanor had realised. She had known pressure for most of her professional life, but the last few days had been like a personal trip to hell on a second-class ticket. It was strange how one's values changed under such circumstances. Saturday afternoon and the whole of Sunday alone had seemed as healing and re-energising as a six-month sabbatical.

Physically and mentally, she felt recharged. She was able to see everything in perspective once again, distinguish reality from nightmare. It was a time when reality seemed important again. Kirsty King was dead, and nothing could bring her back again. John was alone and she was alone — with a career which seemed a thousand times less important than it had all those years ago, when she had needed to prove something to herself.

Above all, it was a time when she felt she could actually talk to John again, discuss a future which did not include all the mistakes of the past.

It was a beautiful day. A starting again day. Monday — start of a week, start of a new era. Eleanor drove with the top down and the side windows wound fully open, enjoying the feeling of freedom. She pulled into Samson's drive, seeing his Range Rover with a sense of relief. The possibility that he might not be at home, perhaps shooting with her father, had been the only thought to cloud her optimism. Eleanor parked beside the Range Rover and stepped out of the Mercedes.

She walked to the front door and pressed the bell. She waited nearly a full minute before trying again, listening carefully for the sound of the doorbell ringing inside the house. It was working perfectly. So why wasn't Samson answering?

Perhaps he was in the back garden, Eleanor thought. She backed away from the front door and walked round the side of the house. The garden was deserted, with no sign that anyone had been working in it recently.

It was strange. She came to the back kitchen door and gently tried the handle. Surprisingly, the door was not locked. Poking her head through the open door, Eleanor called Samson's name. Still there was no answer.

Eleanor's sense of mystery was turning to one of serious concern. Something was very wrong indeed. Samson was not the kind of man who would leave the house with the back door unlocked and the burglar alarm switched off. There were far too many valuables in the house. With a feeling of foreboding, Eleanor crept into the kitchen, closing the door behind her.

The house seemed unnaturally quiet. Eleanor crossed the kitchen, opening the door into the breakfast room. She called out again, listening for the faintest sound of life in return. Nothing. She walked through the breakfast room and opened the door out into the passage. The door of the living room was wide open. She walked down the passage and looked into it. She was totally unprepared for the sight which assaulted her eyes.

Samson's body sat stiffly upright in an armchair. His knees were clenched together with a shotgun wedged between them. His hands lay limply on the triggers. The twin barrels of the gun rested on the shattered remains of his lower jaw. Everything above that was splattered over the wall behind the chair.

Eleanor froze in a helpless terror which was like no stage fright she had ever known. She opened her mouth to scream, but no sound came out. Then even the urge to scream died as vomit rose in her throat. The paralysis passed. Eleanor turned away, ran back along the passage to the kitchen and threw up into the sink.

The forensic team were just finishing off as Taggart and Livingstone came into the room.

Taggart looked at Samson's body dispassionately. "Start of the season," he muttered. Over the years, he'd found his own way of negating the horrors of his job.

Livingstone's experience was more limited. The clinical detatchment with which he had viewed the corpse of Kirsty King deserted him now. The bloody, headless body of Samson churned his stomach and made him feel faint. He turned away, clapping his hand to his mouth and heaved drily.

Taggart was sympathetic. He patted Livingstone's shoulder reassuringly. "Don't ever try and get used to it, Peter. One morning you might wake up and find that nothing affects you any more."

He left the young man to get over it in his own time and busied himself directing the forensic team. He ordered photographs of the gun cabinet, side views of the body and a shot of the blood-spattered wall.

Livingstone had pulled himself together. He forced himself to view the corpse with professional detachment. "Classic suicide postion," he commented.

Taggart shrugged noncommittally and bent down to the gun cabinet, examining the lock.

"No sign that it's been forced," Livingstone said, looking over his shoulder. He glanced quickly round the room. "Or of any kind of a struggle."

"Or of a note," Taggart muttered. He straightened up.

"A popular misconception that, actually," Livingstone said, rather pompously. "In fact, only a minority of suicides leave notes."

Taggart didn't feel like mentioning the number of years he had spent in the force. He arched one eyebrow. "Is that right?" he enquired, with heavy sarcasm. He moved away, checking the catch on the window. It was locked, with no sign of an attempted break-in. Over his shoulder he called to Livingstone. "Go and check all the other windows in the house."

Doctor Andrews arrived as Livingstone was leaving the room. He went straight to the body.

"Bloody mess," Taggart said, joining him.

"I've seen worse," was the reply. Taggart didn't doubt it.

Andrews nodded at the gun. "Twelve bore?"

Taggart nodded.

"Anyone report hearing a shot?"

"Not as far as we know," Taggart told him.

Andrews looked surprised. "Must have made quite a din."

"A car backfiring?" Taggart said with a shrug. "Glasgow's not yet a city where people expect to hear guns going off."

"No, thank goodness," Andrews agreed. He looked at Taggart. "Can I get to work?"

"Aye, he's all yours."

"I'll need to move the gun. OK to touch it?"

Taggart called to the forensic team. "Finished dusting?" Receiving a positive answer he bent down and picked up the gun by its barrel. He deftly cracked open the breech and dug out the two cartridges with his nails. Both had been discharged.

"Both fired," he muttered to himself.

Andrews seemed to think the comment was directed at him. He looked up at the bloodstained wall. "Whatever that means to you," he said.

Livingstone had returned just in time to hear the last comment. "It's a side by side," he volunteered. "You can fire both barrels at the same time."

Taggart looked dubious. "Two cartridges to commit suicide? When one would have done the job just as efficiently." He glanced at Andrews for confirmation.

"Oh, most certainly."

"I wouldn't have thought economy was on his mind at the time," Livingstone put in, facetiously.

Taggart glared at him. "Windows?"

"All locked. No signs of forced entry."

Taggart digested the information. "Right. I'm going to see Mrs Samson," he announced after a while. He turned to Andrews. "Report as soon as possible?"

"Of course." Andrews dived into his bag and pulled out a thermometer. "First of all, let's find out how long he's been dead."

Eleanor Samson sat in the front passenger seat of the police car, staring blankly out through the windscreen. Taggart climbed in beside her, and sat in silence for a few seconds. He noticed that Eleanor's hands were trembling violently. With uncharacteristic gentleness, he reached down and held one. Eleanor did not even seem aware of the gesture.

"I'm sorry," Taggart murmured softly. He paused again before carrying on. "I know things must be very painful for you just now — but I have to ask you some questions."

Eleanor's voice was a husky whisper. "I understand."

"How did you enter the house, Mrs Samson?"

"Through the side door."

"Was it open or closed?"

"Closed. Not locked."

"Why did you come?"

"Just to talk," Eleanor's voice broke on a sob. "I thought it was time."

She was bearing up very well, Taggart thought. He continued to probe gently. "When did you see him last?"

"Not since . . . the fire."

"And Graeme?"

"John threw him out. He's staying with my father. He doesn't know . . ."

"I'll break it as gently as I can," Taggart assured her. He was silent for a long while, testing the mood, sensing the right moment. On nothing but instinct he spoke again, in the same deceptively gentle voice. "Did you kill Kirsty King?"

Eleanor's body stiffened in the car seat. She snatched her hand away from his as though bitten. She whirled to confront him face to face, her expression angry and incredulous. "What a time to ask me that. What kind of a man are you?"

"A policeman, Mrs Samson," Taggart said harshly. "And you're not on stage right now playing the grieving widow. This isn't some big dramatic role. In a few days you may be charged with murder. I want to know *now*. A straight yes or no."

Eleanor closed her eyes, gritting her teeth. "No!" She hissed out the single word with vehemence.

Her anger passed, replaced by confusion and the numbing effect of her recent experience. Taggart felt sure that she was psychologically at her lowest possible ebb. There was no fight left, no need to fight . . . or lie.

Eleanor looked at Taggart's face. There were tears in her eyes. Her expression was almost pleading. "Why won't anyone believe me? I hardly believe myself anymore."

In Taggart's book, she'd passed the test. "I believe you, Mrs Samson," he said softly, and he meant it.

He opened the car door and turned back to face her. "I'll get someone to drive you home." In Eleanor's tear-filled eyes there was a look of gratitude. Taggart knew it wasn't for the offer of a lift.

He got out of the car and walked back towards Samson's house. Andrews was about to leave.

"Well?"

"In my view, suicide. Everything I've seen is totally consistent with that verdict."

Taggart nodded thoughtfully. "Time of death?"

"He's been dead about eight hours. Say between eight-thirty

and ten this morning."

"And no note?" Taggart asked, checking.

Andrews shook his head. "As a matter of fact . . ."

"Only a minority of suicides leave notes," Taggart finished the speech for him. "Yes — somebody has already been good enough to bring that to my attention."

Chapter Thirteen

SAMSON'S body had been removed to the mortuary. The armchair was covered in a plastic bag and a sheet draped against the bloodstained wall. Taggart paced the room, deep in thought. He wasn't at all happy with Andrews' conclusions. It was all too pat. First a murder rigged to look like an accident — now the suicide of the person closest to the victim.

Taggart tried to see things through Samson's eyes. He might have been upset by the news about Kirsty and his son — perhaps even deeply hurt. But mainly, Taggart imagined, he would have been angry . . . and it was his experience that angry people rarely committed suicide. Lonely people, depressed people, desperate people, yes — but someone like Samson? He could buy a dozen Kirsty Kings, if only for a few nights. A man had to have a pretty strong motive to stick a loaded shotgun into his mouth and calmly blow his head off. Try as he might, Taggart just couldn't see the known facts having that effect on a man like John Samson.

What must it feel like? Taggart found himself wondering. He crossed to the gun cabinet and pulled out a shotgun similar to the one found on the body. He opened it, checking that the barrels were empty and carried it over to the chair. He sat down, arranging the gun between his legs and placing the barrel against his lower lip. He reached down for the triggers.

"Don't do it," Livingstone said jokingly, walking into the room.

Taggart looked up sheepishly, lowering the gun. "A man would have to be in a hell of a state of mind to do that for real," he said.

"I can't argue with that," Livingstone agreed. He paused. "I've put a couple of men on to checking the company accounts. See if there was any financial problem."

Taggart was reluctantly impressed. "Good thinking," he said, genuinely. "Are you still going ahead with the report on Eleanor Samson?"

Livingstone was defensive. "McVitie wants me to do it."

"Old Boys' network, is it?" Taggart said scathingly.

Livingstone stared at him, surprise slowly turning to cynical amusement. "I didn't think you knew."

Taggart shook his head reprovingly, "Oh, Peter . . . when are you going to learn? I make it my business to know everything."

Livingstone doubted this, but said nothing. "By the way . . . talking of Mrs Samson. She's come back. Graeme's with her. They want to see you."

Surprised, Taggart stood, putting the shotgun back in the cabinet. "Where are they?"

"I put them in the breakfast room."

"Right. Let's go and see what they have to say." Livingstone accepted the implied invitation and trotted after him.

Eleanor and Graeme were seated as Taggart walked in. Eleanor had used the time to brew a pot of coffee. She offered Taggart and Livingstone a cup, and they accepted. Sipping at the drink, Taggart appraised Graeme over the top of his cup. His red-rimmed eyes showed that he had been crying, but he seemed to be in very good control of himself. Taggart said nothing, waiting for Eleanor to tell him whatever it was she had to say. "Graeme just told me something which I think you ought to know," Eleanor announced at last. She prompted Graeme gently. "Tell the Inspector."

"There's something I didn't tell you," Graeme started out.

"When?" Taggart asked.

"From the very beginning."

Livingstone and Taggart exchanged a glance. "We're listening," Livingstone said.

"Kirsty was still sleeping with Maxwell — her old boss," Graeme announced.

"How do you know that?" Taggart asked.

"She told me herself. She was drunk one night . . . boasting about having three men crazy about her at the same time." Graeme paused for a while, as if unsure whether to go on. "The thing is . . . I told Dad, the night before she was killed. They had a terrible row . . . I heard it all. Dad threatened to kill her."

"Are you sure of this?" Taggart demanded,

"Give me a bible . . . I'll swear on it," Graeme assured him.

"If Graeme says it's true, it is," Eleanor put in.

Taggart thought about it for a while. "How exactly did your father threaten Miss King? What were his exact words?"

"He shouted . . . I'll kill you, you little whore," Graeme said.

"Why didn't you tell us this before?" Livingstone asked. He saw Taggart staring at him and realised what a stupid question it had been.

"You were protecting your father . . . and now there's no point anymore, eh?" Taggart said quietly.

Graeme nodded.

"Why do you think he killed himself, Graeme? Guilt?"

Graeme shook his head. "Not exactly." The boy suddenly seemed secretive, guilty.

"What is it?" Taggart prompted. There was another piece of the puzzle yet to come, he knew.

"The other day . . . after you left. Dad came into my room and told me to get out of the house. I was mad . . . I felt I hated him. I told him I was going to come to you and tell you the whole story."

Taggart understood. "So you think your father killed himself because you were going to expose him . . . and you feel responsible?"

"Yes," Graeme almost screamed the word and broke into tears.

"You're not responsible," Taggart said. "No matter which way it breaks, you did your duty as a son, Graeme, perhaps more than could be expected of you. I want you to know that." He looked over at Eleanor. "Thanks."

"For bringing out the truth? I'm just glad you recognise it when you see it." It was a cryptic comment that Taggart was going to have to think about.

Eleanor stood, urging Graeme to his feet. She looked at Taggart one last time. "If that's all?"

"Yes, of course." Taggart wished he could say more, make more of a gesture. But not in Livingstone's presence.

"Do you think he's telling the truth?" Livingstone asked after they had gone.

"Do you?" Taggart fired the question right back at him.

"Frankly, no."

"Why should he lie?" Taggart mused, as much for himself as for Livingstone.

"To take the heat off his mother."

Taggart nodded slightly, conceding the point. "It's possible."

"But you don't think very probable?" Livingstone was becoming irritated trying to pin his superior down to a definite opinion.

"I think there are still a lot of factors we don't know about," Taggart said.

Livingstone shook his head. He disagreed. "Aren't we in danger of looking deeper into this case than it merits?"

"We, Peter?" Taggart affected surprise. "I thought you and the Biscuit already had it solved."

Taggart had made an excuse to Livingstone about getting home early for a change. Instead, he drove straight to the mortuary, hoping to catch Andrews before he packed up for the night. He only just made it. Andrews was about to climb into his car as Taggart arrived.

He looked up at Taggart peevishly. "If you've come chasing me up about the Samson autopsy . . . the report will be on your desk tomorrow morning."

"Yes and no, Doc," Taggart muttered. "Look, have you got time for a drink?"

Andrews looked disapprovingly. "Never before eight o'clock." He studied Taggart's worried-looking face and relented. "What's your problem?"

Taggart shifted his feet awkwardly. " It's not really a problem. More of a supposition."

"Go on." Andrews waited patiently.

"Suppose someone had knocked Samson unconscious . . . placed him in that chair. The gun is put between his legs, his fingers are wrapped around the triggers . . ."

"And the triggers actually operated by this mysterious third party?" Andrews finished off, catching Taggart's drift.

"Right. Half his head is blown away — obliterating any trace of the first injury."

Andrews considered the proposition very carefully for a while, finally nodding. "Then you would have the perfect murder," he conceded.

Taggart nodded thoughtfully, "Yes . . . that's what I thought," he muttered. He started to walk away, thinking deeply. "Night, Doc," he called over his shoulder.

Chapter Fourteen

BRENNAN'S stomach churned with excitement as he drove to meet Jimmy Petrie, hopefully for the last time. At last, the day had arrived! After nearly a month of planning, making preparations and rehearsing the youth in his precise instructions, he was finally going to do it. Get Lilly out of his life forever and start planning a rosy new future.

Petrie was also day-dreaming of a new future as he waited. Before the day was over he would have committed an act which would make him five thousand pounds richer and would change his life forever.

Over the past two weeks there had been a strange change in his mental attitude. At the beginning, when Brennan had first faced him with the proposition, he had felt trapped by circumstance, pushed into a course of action over which he had no control. Impotence, frustration and anger had all conspired to close in on his mind, compressing his sanity to bursting point. Like a million youngsters before him, the world of fantasy had offered an escape route, and he had taken it gratefully. Now that fantasy had been built upon, embellished, nourished until it took on the trappings of reality. And Petrie's limited brain had accepted it.

Today, a new life began. When Lilly died, so would Jimmy Petrie the no-hope kid in the dole queue. He would kill, and he would get paid for doing it. That made him a professional, a man with a purpose and a future in life. Petrie had it all worked out. He would become a professional hit-man, admired and feared by all who hired him.

He knew it to be possible. Hadn't he seen all the films on television, read about such men in the papers? He had plans. With the five thousand, he would go to London, rent a flat, work his way into the criminal fraternity. In a few years, Petrie told himself, he could be a suave, ruthless killer who travelled the world, accepting only the most dangerous and the most highy paid commissions. He would sun himself on exotic beaches, always with the most beautiful women at his side, unable to resist his ruthless magnetism.

All this was just around the corner. Hooked up in the dream, Petrie's mind did not seek to question why, at that precise moment, he waited on a Glasgow street corner for a publican whose wife he was to batter to death with a hammer.

Brennan turned into the appointed street and slowed to a crawl, looking in the rear-view mirror and out through each side of the car. This was the crucial meeting. No one must see him and Petrie together, be able to make a connection between them at any time in the future. He had made his plans meticulously, worked out each little detail. Nothing must go wrong now, not when he was so close to his dream.

He saw Petrie ahead of him, leaning against a lamp-post, smoking a cigarette. Even from that distance, Brennan noticed there was something different about the youth's pose. There was a swagger, an air of bravado. It was hauntingly familiar. Brennan smiled as he remembered. He had seen it a hundred times in old second-feature cowboy movies.

The street was empty. Petrie saw Brennan's car and pushed himself away from the lamp-post with exaggerated nonchalance. Brennan accelerated up the street, pulling to a stop and throwing open the passenger door. "Get in quick," he hissed.

Petrie climbed in with what he imagined was slow, panther-like elegance. To Brennan it merely looked stupid. He shoved the car into gear and sped off, heading for the outskirts of the city.

They were parked in the same spot Brennan had chosen for their first meeting. For the third time, Petrie repeated the instructions Brennan had rehearsed him in. He was getting bored. It all seemed a far cry from golden guns and beautiful women.

"The hammer is in the drawer under the telephone. The day-room is the first door on the left. I take the hammer, creep into the room where she'll be lying down. I hit her at least twice while she's sleeping then make absolutely sure she's dead. If there's still a heartbeat, or she's breathing, I hit her again . . ." Petrie broke off, looking over at Brennan. "Look, are you sure a rotten bloody hammer is the best weapon you can come up with? Couldn't I shoot her? Couldn't you get a gun from somewhere?"

"Stop being bloody stupid and concentrate," Brennan snapped angrily. "How many times? This has to look like a casual thief caught in a panic — not like a professional job. Know many big-time villains with shooters who go round breaking into scruffy pubs, do you?"

The sarcasm brought Petrie back to earth with a jolt. Wearily, he took up his recitation again. "When I'm sure she's dead, I drag her body over to the telephone, put the receiver in her hand and dial 999."

"Face down," Brennan cut in, irritably. "You must drag her face down. It has to look as though she has crawled to the telephone and made the call herself before she died."

"OK. I drag her body, face down, to the telephone. I dial 999. When the operator answers, I make a croaking sound and say nothing. Then I leave."

"The drawers . . . you forgot about the drawers," Brennan reminded him.

Petrie remembered. "I pull a few drawers out and scatter things on the floor. Make it look like a burglary."

"Right. I'll have already made sure a few things are missing. Now, about the timing. This has to be precise. You enter the pub by the side door at four o'clock exactly. The 999 call will fix the exact time for my alibi."

"Where are you going to be?" Petrie wanted to know.

"That's none of your business," Brennan snapped. "You just do exactly as you've been told and we'll both come out of this as clean as a whistle. Now — go through it one more time."

Petrie groaned, "Do I have to?"

"Yes," Brennan was insistent. "I want to have every detail set in your head. One little change in the plans, one detail missed out could screw the whole thing up."

Wearily, Petrie ran through his script once more. When he'd finished, he looked pleadingly at Brennan. "Is that it, now?"

Brennan considered for a moment. He seemed satisfied. "Right . . . let's synchronise our watches so that the timing is precise."

"I havnae got a watch," Petrie said.

Brennan exploded with anger. "Then how the hell were you going to know when it was four o'clock?" he screamed. He tore at the watch on his own wrist. "Here, take mine."

Petrie slipped the watch on to his own wrist, looking at it. He seemed puzzled. "What's all these figures?"

"Oh God!" Brennan groaned, realising the youth didn't know

how to read a digital watch. Patiently he pointed to the hours, minutes and seconds until Petrie understood. "Now, the last detail," he said finally. "Gloves. You must wear gloves. You've got a record so the police will have your prints on file."

Petrie looked at him scathingly. "Course I'll wear gloves. Do you think I'm stupid or something?"

It wasn't a question Brennan cared to answer at that moment. He reached for the glove compartment and opened it. He pulled out a brown envelope. "Here's half of the money as we agreed. You'll get the second half in two weeks time, after the hue and cry has died down a bit. You are to make no effort to see me or contact me in any way. Do you understand that?"

"Aye," Petrie said. "How do I get the second lot of money?"

Brennan smiled to himself. The youth was canny enough when it came to important things. He gestured to the envelope. "In there with the first instalment is an exact location. Go there in two weeks time and follow the instructions. The money will be there waiting for you."

Petrie seemed a little unhappy about this arrangement. For the first time in his dealing with Brennan he showed signs of aggression. "It had better be . . . or I'll come looking for you, mister."

Brennan had no doubt that he would. He had never doubted it, or underestimated the youth's potential for violence. That was why he had been chosen for the job, and why it should work. Brennan had no intentions of spoiling things by reneging on the contract. "Just check the money, will you?" he said. "It's important that we trust each other."

Petrie opened the envelope. Inside was a wad of one hundred and twenty-five £20 notes. He regarded them in awe. The dream of being an international assassin suddenly seemed very real again, even if cold reality did still try to claw its way in. "You are sure she'll be asleep?" Petrie asked, his voice shaky.

"I'm certain. She always takes a nap at that time. I've checked her every day since I first planned this."

"So nothing can go wrong?" Petrie seemed to need that last piece of reassurance.

"Nothing can go wrong. Nothing *will* go wrong," Brennan said firmly.

It was enough. The international assassin gave his first client a cool, confident professional smile. "I'll do a good job for you."

Brennan started the car, feeling exhilarated. He had no doubt of it.

Chapter Fifteen

THE two women stood behind the bar of the Firhill, cleaning glasses. "I think you're doing the right thing, dear," Olive said to Lilly. "Like I told you, my Jack suffered agonies with varicose veins for years, but he didn't do anything about it."

"Well, it's just a preliminary consultancy," Lilly said. "They'll tell me whether or not I need surgery. Then I'll have to think about it again."

The telephone rang. Lilly went to answer it. When she came back she looked worried.

"Anything wrong, dear?" Olive asked solicitously.

"That was the brewery," Lilly announced. "The draymen want to deliver today instead of tomorrow."

Olive understood the problem. "What time's your appointment?"

"Quarter to four," Lilly told her.

Olive smiled. "Don't worry, Lilly. I can stay on for a couple of hours. As I said . . . I can always do with the extra money."

"Are you sure?" Lilly looked uncertain.

"Of course, dear." Olive looked down at her watch. "Come on now — away with you. You'll be late."

"Well . . . thank you, Olive." Lilly went to get her coat. She came back with an afterthought. "Oh, by the way . . . don't tell Keith where I've gone if he comes back while I'm out. I haven't told him I'm going privately. He'd only moan about the expense."

"I shan't say a word, dear," Olive assured her. As Lilly walked away, she made a little joke to cheer her up. "Enjoy having your legs felt, Lilly. I wish a man would feel mine sometimes."

Lilly smiled thinly. The joke wasn't quite to her taste. She got to the front door and checked her watch. It was half-past three. If the bus was on time, she should make her appointment with no trouble.

Brennan walked unhurriedly down the road towards the shopping precinct. He'd checked the clock above the jeweller's shop by the bank and knew he had a couple of minutes to play with. He stopped to buy an evening newspaper from the stand, making a great play out of only having a five-pound note to change. Continuing along the street towards the dry-cleaning shop, he deliberately bumped into a couple of people and made profuse apologies. The more people who remembered his presence in the precinct at that time, the better.

He reached the dry-cleaning shop and paused, arranging the two suits he was carrying over his arm. Satisfied, he strolled into the shop to fix his alibi.

Brennan's face fell as he opened the door. There were two customers already waiting, and Dorothy was nowhere to be seen. A brief moment of panic passed, as Brennan pulled himself together. He was getting jumpy — a silly mistake. It was most important that he acted perfectly naturally. Obviously, Dorothy had gone out to the back of the shop to fetch something.

He stepped into the shop, joining the queue. He could hear Dorothy's voice from out the back, speaking to someone. Presumably she was on the telephone.

Brennan's eyes strayed up to the clock upon the wall — the clock with which he had intended to set his alibi. Again, a brief spasm of panic shook him as he realised that the clock was broken, registering ten past nine. In sudden desperation he prodded the man in front of him in the back. "Excuse me, but do you have the correct time?"

The man turned, an apology on his lips. "Sorry, I don't wear a watch."

Brennan recognised him. It was Mulholland. They had met only the once, some years ago, when Mulholland had been interested in purchasing the Firhill site.

Mulholland's eyes were dull, disinterested. He didn't recognise Brennan. Brennan could find no valid reason to reintroduce himself. He just muttered: "Thanks anyway."

Mulholland turned back to face the counter as Dorothy emerged from the rear of the shop and attended to the female customer. "I'm sorry. I've just been on to the suede cleaning people and they promise the jacket will be here the day after tomorrow. Again. sorry about the delay."

The customer turned, disgruntled, and stormed out of the shop. Mulholland moved up, laying a tweed jacket on the. counter. Brennan edged up beside him to the counter, anxious that

Dorothy should acknowledge him. She saw him, flashed a little smile.

"Just this jacket," Mulholland said.

Dorothy took out a docket pad and started to write. She paused, looking up at him. "I was sorry to hear about your son-in-law," she said.

Mulholland said nothing. Dorothy continued to look up at him, smiling gently. "Haven't seen you for some while," she went on. "How are you?"

Brennan was beginning to get nervous and fidgety. He just wanted Mulholland out of the shop so he could fix that all-important time. He had already seen the strap of a wristwatch on Dorothy's arm. Why was she wasting precious time? Brennan asked himself. It was as if she were deliberately trying to establish familiarity with Mulholland — and none too subtly. He quite obviously did not know her, and was in no mood to banter small talk. "When will the jacket be ready?" Mulholland asked.

Dorothy switched off the smile. "Day after tomorrow do?"

"Fine," Mulholland said with a nod. As Dorothy began to write out the ticket, he began to spell his name. "That's M-U-L-H . . ."

Dorothy cut in, somewhat abruptly. "I do know." She finished writing out the ticket, tore it off and handed it to him. Mulholland left the shop with a slightly puzzled look on his face.

Brennan threw the two suits over the counter. He made a quick pretence of noticing the stopped clock. "Hullo — your clock's on the blink, Dot. What time is it, anyway?"

Dorothy glanced at her wrist. "It's just four o'clock," she told him.

"Good Lord!" Brennan said. " I had no idea it was so late. My wife will kill me if I don't get back by opening time."

Petrie had decided that one of his first purchases would be a digital watch. Professional people needed accurate timekeeping, since time was money. Besides, he liked the way the seconds flashed off, the liquid crystal figures changing like magic. It still took a bit of working out, knowing that 3:59:09 meant nearly one minute to four, but he was sure he would get the hang of it after a while. He probably hadn't learned to read a proper clock face right away.

He kept staring at the watch face as the seconds flashed by, finally jumping from 59 back to two zeros. As Brennan had explained to him, the important figure, the one on the left now read four o'clock.

He set out across the patch of derelict land at the rear of the pub, looking around him carefully. Just as Brennan had promised, the area was deserted. Petrie reached the side door, and gently tried the handle. It opened as smoothly as silk. Petrie slipped inside quickly, congratulating himself. So far, everything was going exactly according to plan.

He crept up the stairs to the flat, pausing on the landing to remember his next move. A slight moment of panic as he realised he had forgotten something. He struggled to remember. Had Brennan told him to ransack the flat before or after he got the hammer out from the drawer by the telephone? With a flash of relief it came to him. Afterwards, on the way out. First he had to go down the stairs to the bar. Killing the woman at exactly four o'clock was the first priority. The telephone was in the passage. The day-room was the first door on the left. The woman would be sleeping. It would be quick, and easy. No screaming, no struggling. Just a couple of quick blows and he was halfway to those holiday paradise spots his mother dreamed about.

Petrie ran all these things through his mind, hoping they would quell the rising sense of nausea in his guts. Perhaps it got easier with the second and third times. Perhaps one day he really would be able to kill with a cold, sadistic precision. Certainly he didn't want this trembling feeling in his legs every time he went to work. The horribly loud thumping sound of his own heart beating. The fear.

The international assassin was fading quickly, the dream fraying out at the edges and curling off into the smoky mist that dreams are made of. Petrie inched his way down the flight of stairs which led to the bar, saw the telephone and crept towards it. He opened the top drawer slowly and carefully, dreading the slightest squeak.

He stared at the metal claw hammer with detached curiosity. It was like some weird alien instrument he had never seen before. He picked it up by its rubber-sheathed handle, weighing it in his hand, imagining the effect it would have on the brittle bone of a human skull.

The dream vanished completely, in a few last wisps of

evaporating steam. There was just an ill-educated kid, standing in a strange hallway, with a hammer in his hand and murder on his mind. Petrie froze in indecision, not knowing what to do. He wondered what Brennan would do if he let him down. What *could* he do? The photographs? Those damned photographs!

In a reflex gesture of frustration, Petrie slammed the drawer shut, regretting the stupid move even as his hand did the work. The sound seemed to reverberate through the empty hallway like a thunder clap. In the silence which followed, Petrie's pulsing heart boomed out like jungle drums.

Olive heard the dull thud of the closing drawer from inside the bar. She paused in the act of loading bottles on to the shelves and straightened up, listening intently. She called out.

"Keith — is that you?" Brennan sometimes sneaked in the back way to avoid Lilly.

There was no answer. Perhaps it was a door banging, Olive thought. In total innocence, she went to investigate.

Petrie heard the sound of the door opening and whirled towards it, a look of terror on his face. He raised the hammer, in a gesture of self-defence.

Olive didn't have time to feel fear. Surprise froze her in the doorway, regarding the young intruder with the strange look in his eyes. He was just a boy, perhaps a year or two younger than her own son, and he was in trouble. Maternal instinct made her take that one fatal step towards him.

Petrie shook his head wildly, moaning, "No . . . no." He just wanted her to turn away, leave him to make his escape. Things had all gone terribly wrong, and now all he wanted was a chance to run. He glanced fearfully over his shoulder, realising that he was backed into a corner by the telephone, with Olive blocking both possible escape routes. There was another brief moment in which they both froze, regarding each other.

Then Petrie ran at her, hoping that she would move out of his way. She didn't. He lashed out wildly with the hammer, catching her across the side of the head, just above the eye. Olive's legs buckled. She fell against him, her arms already raised in a late defence against the hammer blow. To Petrie in his panic it seemed that she was trying to grab hold of his throat, pull him down. He struck downwards with the hammer three more times, backing off as she finally slithered to the floor and lay there, unmoving.

Petrie stared at her head in horror. Blood was pulsing out in rhythmic little spurts, soaking quickly into the Berber-style carpet. The instinct to run was uppermost in his mind, but Brennan's instructions had been drummed into his mind. Like a trained animal, he performed without thinking. Even though it was the wrong victim, Petrie moved to the phone, dialled 999 and let the receiver dangle on its cord. Then, stepping back over Olive's body, he ran out the way he had come, dropping the hammer on the stairs.

Outside, he raced back across the waste land, slowing down and stopping only as a road came into view. He looked at his gloves, shuddering as he saw they were heavily bloodstained. He peeled them off, hurriedly, crumpled them into a ball and threw them away. On an afterthought, he remembered Brennan's watch and slid it from his wrist, dropping it and walking away.

Chapter Sixteen

TAGGART drove into the police station car park and eased into his reserved space. He switched off the engine and started to climb out. Livingstone came racing out of the door and across to him.

"There's been a murder at the Firhill Tavern."

Taggart settled back in his seat, leaned across and released the lock on the passenger door. "Who?" he asked as Livingstone got in.

"A woman. In the living quarters," Livingstone said.

Taggart groaned. He was genuinely upset. "Aw no . . . not Lilly."

Livingstone could only shrug. He had given Taggart all the information at his disposal. He could understand how his superior felt. Murder was obscene under any circumstances. But when it came close . . .

The police photographer was already there. The forensic team had yet to arrive. Taggart looked down at the body, glad it wasn't Lilly, sorry it was somebody else.

"Who found the body?" he asked one of the two young constables present.

"We were directed here by the emergency services, sir. Seems there was a 999 call."

Taggart looked down at the position of the body again, and over to the telephone still dangling from its cord. "Well she couldn't have made the call from there, that's for sure." He moved back towards the stairs, looking around.

"Murder weapon's up there, sir. Fifth step," one of the constables called. "It's not been touched."

Taggart walked up the stairs, taking a plastic evidence bag from one pocket and a clean paper tissue from the other. He bent down, using the tissue to pick up the hammer, just under the head. He dropped it into the bag, turned and came back down the stairs.

Livingstone was looking at the telephone receiver, without touching it. "There's a bloodstain on the receiver. Smudgy . . .

114

looks like it might have been made with a woven glove. Looks like the killer didn't mean her to die."

Taggart waved the plastic bag in the air. "What do you think he was trying to do then? Hang up a bloody picture?"

Livingstone was unabashed. "Perhaps she was still alive when he made the call."

Taggart looked disgusted. "I thought you'd outgrown that stage."

"What stage?" Livingstone didn't understand.

"Laying the groundwork for the defence," Taggart retorted, turning away to give instructions to the photographer.

Brennan saw the police car parked outside the front entrance and smiled happily. So it was done. It was all over. He parked his car round the side of the building and took a few minutes to practice a deeply concerned expression in the mirror. Satisfied with it, he stepped out of the car and braced himself for his encounter with the police.

A single constable stood on duty outside the door. He raised his hand as Brennan approached. "Sorry, sir. You can't go in there for the present."

"But I live here. This is my pub," Brennan protested.

The constable looked apologetic. "Sorry, sir. I must warn you though — there's been a murder."

Brennan opened his mouth to speak, and pulled himself up sharp in the nick of time. He felt a cold prickle up his back. He had been about to say, "yes, I know". Instead, he let his mouth drop open slackly, in what he imagined was a suitable expression of horrified surprise. "Oh, my God!" he blurted out after a second, and pushed his way past the constable and through the door.

Lilly was waiting for him, sitting at one of the tables just inside the door. Brennan's mouth dropped open again, but this time he wasn't acting. "Lilly . . . what the . . ."

"It's Olive, Keith. She's been murdered." Lilly's voice broke on a sob. She rose from her seat and ran to him, holding out her arms to be embraced and comforted. Brennan took her in his arms, feeling physically sick, and mentally troubled. He'd liked Olive, and was deeply upset at the tragic, stupid mistake. He was also wondering whether Petrie would give him his two and half thousand pounds back.

The body was gone, and a sheet draped over the bloodstains and chalked figure on the carpet. Taggart drew four chairs up to a table in the bar and invited Lilly and Brennan to sit down. He and Livingstone sat opposite.

"It would have been me, if I hadn't gone to see that specialist," Lilly murmured, still shaken.

Brennan nodded, keeping his thoughts on that particular score to himself.

"That's the way it goes sometimes, Lilly," Taggart said. He turned to Brennan. "How long have you known Mrs MacQueen?"

"Oh . . . years," Brennan told him.

"She used to come in almost every night with her husband — until he died," Lilly volunteered. "I got friendly with her and offered her a part-time job."

"Any other relations that you know of?" Livingstone enquired.

"There's a sister living somewhere in England," Brennan offered.

"Brighton," Lilly expanded. Livingstone took notes.

"Purely as a matter of procedure, Keith . . . where were you at four o'clock this afternoon?" Taggart asked.

"I was at the dry cleaners — Quality Dry — in the precinct."

Lilly turned to face him, suspicion on her face and in her voice. "What did you go there for? We sent all the cleaning a couple of days ago."

Brennan kept calm, affecting a shrug. "There were a couple of my suits I thought looked a bit shabby."

Taggart looked at him apologetically. "We'll have to check it out, Keith. Like I said — just procedure."

Brennan forced a smile. "I should hope so, Mr Taggart. I mean — you don't suspect me, do you?"

Taggart smiled back, "Course not, Keith." He stood up. "Right — that's it for now. I'd like you both to go upstairs and make a full list of any missing items, if you will."

"Yes, of course," Brennan got up, helping Lilly to her feet. She looked surprised. The pair disappeared upstairs.

Taggart turned to Livingstone. "Check out Keith's story, will you?"

"Do you suspect him?" Livingstone asked.

Taggart shrugged noncommittally. "He wouldn't be the first

bird to shit in his own nest."

The dry-cleaning shop was empty as Livingstone walked in. He pulled his ID card from his pocket, showing it to Dorothy.

"Afternoon. We're just running a routine check. Can you tell me if you had a customer called Brennan in the shop this afternoon? Keith Brennan?"

Dorothy reached for her docket book. "I'll have a look for you." Suddenly, she remembered, and pushed the book aside. "Oh, you mean Keith the photographer? Oh yes, he was in here. He comes here a lot. Usually it's things for his wife, but today he brought in a couple of suits." She paused, looking at Livingstone inquisitively. "What's he done?"

"He's done nothing, as far as we know," Livingstone said firmly. "Can you remember what time he was in?"

Dorothy nodded emphatically. "Oh yes. It was four o'clock exactly."

"You seem very sure."

"He asked me the time," Dorothy said. She gestured up to the stopped clock, which still read ten-past nine. "I keep forgetting to get a new battery."

"You own the shop, do you?" Livingstone asked.

"Yes."

"Can I just have your name, please." Livingstone took out his notebook.

Dorothy was about to answer when something caught her eye outside the shop door. A woman customer was just about to come in. Dorothy moved quickly, ducking out from behind the counter and slipping the door lock into position. She flipped over the 'Closed' sign, ignoring the angry glare from the customer. Livingstone turned just as she was walking away in disgust. He caught only a glimpse of her head.

"Listen, you don't have to close up on my account," he told Dorothy. "I was just leaving . . . once I took your name."

"It's Milner — Dorothy Milner." She put on a smile. "It's almost closing time anyway. I want to get away a bit sharpish this evening."

"I won't keep you, then," Livingstone returned the smile and turned to the door. Dorothy unlatched it and let him out, closing it quickly behind him. She *was* in a hurry, Livingstone thought.

"This yours, Keith?" Taggart laid the digital watch down on the bar counter.

Brennan stared at it in confusion. Caught on the hop like that, he didn't know whether to identify it or not. He played for time to give his racing mind time to concentrate. "I'm not sure."

Lilly came hurrying along the bar, curious. She looked at the watch, recognising it at once. "That's the one I bought you for your birthday," she said to Brennan. Then, looking at Taggart: "Where did you find it?"

"Out in the waste ground behind the pub," Taggart said. "So it *is* yours, Keith. You didn't seem too sure."

"They all look pretty much alike," Brennan bluffed. To his relief Taggart agreed with him.

"Aye — like too many things these days."

"You didn't list it as missing," Livingstone put in suddenly. Brennan thought quickly. "I didn't really miss it."

"Yet you asked the time in the dry cleaners yesterday." Livingstone jumped on the inconsistency at once.

Brennan was getting rattled. "I thought I'd left it in my darkroom," he blurted out, feeling pleased with himself. Livingstone went off the boil.

"Anyway, we got a nice print off it," Taggart announced. Brennan felt his guts tighten. "Print?"

"A fingerprint. He must have thrown away the gloves, and the watch afterwards. With your positive identification of the watch, we've got the little bastard."

Brennan hoped that the fear he felt didn't show on his face. "You've got someone? That was quick."

Taggart shrugged. "Some come easy. This one did. The kid has a record. All we have to do is pick him up."

"Kid?" Brennan repeated, dully.

"A laddie named Jimmy Petrie. Lives not too far from here. Name mean anything to you?"

Both Brennan and Lilly shook their heads. Taggart shrugged again. "Just thought he might have drunk in here some times."

Livingstone had picked up the watch and was reading the manufacturer's name. "It's not a cheap one," he observed.

"I should think not," Lilly said, indignantly.

Livingstone explained. "What I mean is — it seems odd that a burglar should throw it away, only seconds after he had stolen it. If it was one of the cheap and nasty digital watches available, I could understand it."

"Perhaps he already had a watch," Brennan suggested. Anything to take the pressure off.

The argument carried no weight, but Livingstone let it go.

"Anyway, we'll keep you posted," Taggart said. "We'll have to keep the watch for now, if you don't mind."

"No, that's fine," Brennan said, trying to sound as casual as possible.

Taggart started to move away from the bar, then turned on an afterthought. "Oh, by the way . . ." Brennan tensed himself, half-expecting another little bombshell. ". . . You'll be glad to know that we managed to contact Mrs MacQueen's sister. She'll be making all the arrangements."

"Oh, good," Brennan said, heaving an inward sigh of relief. He promised himself a very large Scotch the moment Taggart walked out through the door.

Outside, Taggart checked the Petrie address thrown up by Criminal Records. "Right — let's go get him." He and Livingstone climbed into the car.

Livingstone turned to him with a thoughtful look on his face. "Did you think that Keith Brennan seemed nervous?"

Taggart thought about it, finally shrugging it off with a laugh. "Oh, he's always like that. Can't be a barrel of laughs, living with Lilly. Besides, he was probably extra worried because he hadn't noticed her birthday present was missing."

The explanation made sense. Livingstone seemed mollified. "Bit of a harridan then, is she . . . Lilly?"

Taggart grinned. "Oh, aye." He started the car and drove off.

Mrs Petrie answered the door. Taggart and Livingstone already had their ID cards out, displaying them.

"Polis? What do you want?" The woman sounded aggressive. She knew, Taggart thought.

"I think you know what we want, Mrs Petrie. Where's Jimmy?"

"Not here."

"Mind if we come in?" Taggart was over the threshold before he'd finished speaking. Livingstone followed him in and

119

immediately started checking the rooms. Taggart walked into the sitting room.

"Where was Jimmy yesterday afternoon, Mrs Petrie? About four o'clock?" Taggart demanded.

The woman was a poor liar. Her eyes gave her away as she spoke. "Here, with me."

"Are you sure?"

The woman pointed to a small crucifix mounted on the wall. "As He's my witness."

Livingstone walked into the room. "No sign of him," he said. Hardly had the words left his mouth before they heard the sound of a door slamming. It was definitely the sound of someone going out, not coming in.

"Damn!" Livingstone cursed. "He must have been hiding in a cupboard or something." He made a break for the door, off in pursuit.

Taggart stayed where he was. He was too well aware of his physical limitations to go haring after 18-year-olds. He looked at Mrs Petrie with a strange, almost pitying smile on his face. He couldn't blame her for trying to protect her son — whatever he'd done. He nodded slightly towards the crucifix. "He'll forgive you, Mrs Petrie. I hope He'll forgive your son as well."

Taggart walked out of the flat and stood on the balcony. He saw Petrie emerge from the ground floor and start racing across the tarmac towards some derelict buildings. Seconds later Livingstone came out and set off in hot pursuit. "Fit little bugger," he thought. He set out after them at a leisurely pace.

Petrie's advantages from muscle-building were offset by his heavy smoking. He was already short of breath by the time he reached the outside of the flats, and he had no idea how to properly pace his running. Livingstone, on the other hand, had build and stamina on his side, and a sports background which had included plenty of cross-country running. He loped, rather than ran, head well up, chest out, drawing his breath in rhythmic, energy-conserving lungfuls. With every stride he was closing the gap between him and his quarry.

Petrie glanced over his shoulder a couple of times, and realised this fact for himself. There was no way he could outrun the tall, wiry young copper on his tail. Changing direction slightly, he headed for a block of derelict and condemned flats, knowing from experience where to find a vandalised gap in the perimeter fence. Coming to the hole, he threw himself under it, scrambled to his feet and dragged himself, panting, towards the first entrance he could see.

Livingstone reached the wire and paused, just long enough to read the notice which hung from it at an odd angle.

WARNING!
GUARD DOGS ON REGULAR PATROL
VANDALS WILL BE PROSECUTED

He shrugged to himself, and rolled under the wire.

Inside the block, Petrie realised he had trapped himself, running into a dead end. All of the flats were heavily boarded up. The only place to run was up the concrete stairs. When they ran out, four floors up, the only way back to ground level was the express route, out of a window.

On the second-floor level Petrie pulled himself into a shadowy corner under a dog-leg in the stairs and rested, struggling to catch his breath and listening for Livingstone at the same time.

Livingstone came through the entrance carefully, wary of an ambush. In the small foyer area by the sealed and disconnected lifts, he looked around him, and assessed the situation in a matter of seconds. He relaxed, knowing the chase was over. He took a few slow, deep breaths to recharge himself in case the kid decided to make a fight of it.

He moved to the bottom of the first flight of stairs and called up. "It's over, Jimmy. There's no way out. Come down and give yourself up."

There was no answer. Livingstone had not really expected one. He held his breath for a second, listening intently. Was it his imagination, or could he hear the faint sound of heavy breathing coming from the landing above him?

A full minute passed, but Livingstone was in no hurry. Time could only work against Petrie, alone in a hopeless situation. He would either give up in despair, or attempt an escape in panic. There was no other choice. Either way, he had to come to Livingstone.

He chose the latter course eventually. Livingstone heard the faint sound of shoes scuffing against concrete and braced himself at the bottom of the stairs. Petrie appeared at the top, glaring down at Livingstone defiantly, weighing up his chances in a hand-to-hand struggle.

"Don't even think about it, Jimmy," Livingstone mocked, trying to break whatever spirit the kid had left in him.

"I can take you," Petrie tried to sound menacing, but there was no conviction in his voice.

"Try it," Livingstone invited.

Petrie eased down a couple of stairs, preparing himself for a full-bodied charge. Livingstone tensed himself, rehearsing a low tackle at the youth's ankles.

A voice behind Livingstone made him whirl, startled. A security guard stood just inside the entrance, holding a very large and very ferocious-looking Alsatian on a short chain leash. "What do you think you're doing?"

Livingstone cast a quick, nervous glance up at Petrie, who was about to make his break. He glanced back at the security guard, who was just bending over to release the dog. Livingstone screamed. "No . . . I'm a police officer." He dived into his pocket for his card.

The move was misinterpreted. The guard snapped off the leash, slapped the dog on the haunches as an attack signal. "Go, Bruce."

As the dog headed for Livingstone, Petrie tensed himself for a dash to freedom. He couldn't believe his luck.

Livingstone threw his arm up in self-defence as the Alsatian leapt into the attack. The dog seized his forearm between its massive jaws, shaking, worrying in the way it had been trained. Livingstone forced himself to stop struggling, knowing it was the only way to avoid serious injury. Above him, Petrie made his move, running down the stairs and using the banister to vault clear over Livingstone and the dog. He burst past the security guard and sprinted through the exit . . . only to trip over the leg Taggart casually extended in his way at ankle level. Petrie went flying, crashing to the ground in an awkward, body-slamming fall which knocked the last bit of fight out of him. He lay there meekly as Taggart stepped over, pulled his arms behind his back and snapped cuffs over his wrists.

Livingstone emerged from the flats, holding his arm in pain. He looked pale and shaken. Behind him, the security guard trotted sheepishly, the dog once more on the leash. Livingstone ignored them, as he tried to disregard the guard's whining apology.

"Sorry, honest . . . but I thought you were one of the glue-sniffers we get in here."

Livingstone glared at Taggart, almost taunting him to display the slightest indication of amusement. His face was a mask. Livingstone found this equally infuriating, but said nothing.

Taggart offered an olive branch. He nodded down at Petrie, now sitting up. "Your collar, Peter."

Livingstone didn't thank him for the gesture. He figured he'd earned it.

Chapter Seventeen

PETRIE stared gloomily at the neatly typed confession in front of him. Partial confession, that was, since he had retained the canny sense to keep quiet about his involvement with Brennan. Even someone with his limited intelligence realised that a jury might make some allowance for a young offender who had killed, inadvertently, in a moment of panic. Those same twelve just men and true would doubtless take a very different view of someone who plotted, coldbloodedly over several weeks, to take a human life for a few month's wages.

"Well — have you read it?" Taggart asked, prompting the youngster for some display of life.

"Yes." Petrie said the word flatly. It was a lie. His eyes had merely skimmed the paper the words were typed on, not noticing even the spaces between them. He had told his story, and he assumed the Police had taken it all down faithfully. He was past caring, or at least past comprehending what was happening to him.

"Are you going to sign it?" Livingstone asked, proffering a ball-point pen.

Taggart produced his own fountain pen, pulling off the cap with a flourish. "No — let him use my good pen." He thrust the pen into Petrie's fingers where it hung, motionless, poised over the incriminating text. Taggart waited, patiently, knowing the frightening psychological barrier confronting the lad.

"How many years will I get?" Petrie's voice was almost a croak.

"For manslaughter? Oh . . . three, maybe four." Taggart was deliberately casual, reducing the crime almost to the level of a childish prank.

Petrie was not convinced. "But you're charging me with murder."

Taggart nodded, his face serious, but reassuring. "I know that, Jimmy . . . but we don't have any choice, you see. A court'll see things differently, you see. You didn't mean to kill her. You made that 999 call. A jury will look sympathetically on that . . . won't they, Peter?"

Taggart turned suddenly on Livingstone, who was rubbing at his injured arm, wincing slightly. The sudden question caught him off balance. "Oh . . . yes, certainly," Livingstone muttered, without any conviction in his voice.

It didn't matter. Petrie had no choice, and he knew it. He pressed the pen down to the confession, and with a slightly trembling hand, signed it.

Taggart's attitude changed at once. He looked over to the uniformed policeman standing by the door and snapped his fingers, gesturing to Petrie. "Take him away."

Taggart did not give the youth a second look as the constable escorted him off to the cells.

"Why did you lie to him?" Livingstone asked.

Taggart shrugged carelessly. "I don't believe in time wasting. Anyway, it may just work out that way. Some of the ludicrous sentences the courts hand out these days."

He looked at Livingstone's arm, noticing the bulge of heavy bandages under the shirt. "How is your arm, anyway?"

"Painful. But no doubt it will be better by the weekend."

"Oh. Something important this weekend, is it?" Taggart feigned innocence.

"I'm taking Alison out again . . . as you well know."

"Oh . . . aye! She *did* mention something about it, now that you remind me. Must have slipped my mind. Ah, well it's nice you two are getting on so well."

Taggart sounded so genuine. Livingstone took the bait like a hungry mackerel. "Do you mean that?" He knew he had come second in one of Taggart's little games as soon as he saw the smirk appearing on his superior's face.

"Of course. I'd hate to think she was hanging around with glue-sniffing types, Peter."

Taggart delivered the punchline and made a break for the door, mightily pleased with his little quip. Livingstone glared after him, failing to find anything remotely funny in it.

The telephone rang. Livingstone snatched it up testily. "Yes?"

Taggart froze in the doorway, his expression vaguely curious.

Livingstone listened for several seconds before putting down the receiver. He looked across at Taggart with a slightly mischievous sense of intrigue.

"Well?" Taggart said.

"It's Mulholland," Livingstone announced.

"What about him?" Taggart found mysteries irritating.

Livingstone waited, timing his answer with the precision of a Shakespearean actor.

"He's been found dead." Livingstone delivered the words deadpan and kept his face expressionless as he savoured the rare pleasure of wiping that annoying smirk from Taggart's face.

Doctor MacNaughton was waiting for them when they arrived. He showed them into Mulholland's living room, pointing to the body on the floor. "I haven't moved him. He was dead when I arrived."

Taggart viewed the body dispassionately, and sniffed the air. The faint acrid smell of charred flesh was unmistakeable. He looked again at Mulholland's body. It lay slumped across the hearth-rug, against the electric fire. Mulholland appeared to have toppled forward from his armchair. There was an overturned glass some feet away from his outstretched hand and a half-empty bottle of Calvados still upright beside the chair.

"Who found the body?" Taggart asked.

"Graeme," MacNaughton said. "He telephoned me and I came straight round. I called you at once."

"Why? Suspicious circumstances?" Livingstone enquired.

MacNaughton shrugged. "Not at all. But any sudden death ..."

Taggart nodded, interrupting. "Opinion?"

"Cause of death? Cardiac arrest, almost certainly. As I believe I once told you, he had a history."

Taggart stepped forward, peering over the body. The source of the burning smell was immediately obvious. The whole of Mulholland's right side was seared, right through to the ribs.

MacNaughton read Taggart's unspoken thoughts. "The way I see it, he felt an attack coming on, made the effort to rise from the chair and collapsed on to the fire. One bar was on, Graeme told me. He switched the fire off."

"An electric fire? In August?" Livingstone sounded sceptical.

"Old people feel the cold," MacNaughton told him. He gestured down to the Calvados bottle. "That wouldn't have helped. Warms you inside, but causes sweating and evaporation which drains body heat. I did warn him about drinking."

"How long has he been dead?" Taggart asked.

"Judging from the degree of burning, I'd say about five or six hours. Graeme found him when he came home from school at four-thirty, so he'd probably been lying there since mid-morning. Of course, I'll give you an accurate time when I've had a chance to examine him more thoroughly. I'll make all the arrangements, sign the death certificate, of course."

"That won't be necessary," Taggart said.

MacNaughton looked at him in surprise. "I don't understand."

"The police surgeon will be giving us a full autopsy report."

"But I told you . . . it's death from natural causes. Good God, man — I know my job and I know my patient. I've been expecting this day for the past three years."

"I'll give you credit for knowing your job if you'll give me credit for knowing mine," Taggart retorted, bristling slightly. "And my copper's nose tells me that there have been too many sudden deaths in this family to stretch coincidence. And I hate coincidence anyway."

MacNaughton looked astonished. "You're going to treat this as *murder*?"

Taggart nodded. "Until someone gives me a better idea . . . and proves it." He paused, letting his words sink in. "Now — where's Graeme?"

"He went to tell his mother. It might be sensitive if you could leave them alone until the morning, at least."

Taggart sneered at him. "Do I look the sensitive type?" He turned to Livingstone. "Go and bring Graeme in for questioning. And try not to upset Mrs Samson," he added, on afterthought.

Livingstone made his departure. Taggart looked around the room carefully. His eyes fell on the open flap of a writing bureau. He walked over to it, looking at a pile of bank statements and papers lying there.

"Any idea how much he was worth?"

"You mean money?"

"I'm not talking about scrap value," Taggart snorted, sarcastically. "He was a wealthy man, wasn't he? Wealthy men always have people who'd prefer them dead."

MacNaughton gave Taggart a pitying smile. "So that's how a man's worth is measured in your book, is it?"

Taggart ignored the accusation. "No, in a killer's book," he said quietly.

Chapter Eighteen

EVEN in a professional capacity, Taggart felt slightly ill at ease in a bank manager's office. He fidgeted in his chair as he and Livingstone waited for Pearson to extract the relevant papers from the files. Livingstone noticed his superior's discomfort and took the opportunity to get in a quick jibe. He was learning, fast. "Worried about your overdraft?"

Taggart flashed him a scathing look and busied himself toying with the brass name-plate on Pearson's desk.

The manager returned, at last. He had a large manilla envelope in his hand. Seating himself, he drew out the contents carefully, laying the papers out on his desk. He selected a thin sheaf of neatly typewritten papers and passed them across to Taggart.

"This is Mr Mulholland's will. Received by us on the twelfth of August."

Livingstone exchanged a quick glance with Taggart and got the words in first. "Start of the season," he observed.

Taggart started to read the will. Pearson extracted another single sheet, also typewritten, and handed it to Livingstone. "And this is the letter we received with the will, asking for early confirmation."

Livingstone read through the letter carefully. There was a slightly thoughtful frown on his brow as he looked up at Pearson again. "Is it normal to deposit a will direct with a bank without going through a solicitor?"

Pearson gave a slight shrug. "It's not normal ... but then it's not unusual, either. A lot of people just object to paying a solicitor's fees."

Taggart had been listening while he read the will. "Even someone with his money?" he put in.

Pearson grinned wryly. "Especially someone with his money. Nobody ever got rich giving it away."

"How rich?" Taggart wanted to know.

Pearson considered for a while. "Well — with investments, the house, shares in the company ... I'd say on the better side of three million."

Taggart whistled through his teeth. "Makes my pension look a bit sick," he muttered. He passed the will over to Livingstone. "Read it. Tell me your first reactions."

Livingstone pored through the text for several moments.

Taggart prompted him as he read. "A typed will . . . signed by Mulholland . . . and witnessed by John Samson and Kirsty King . . ."

"Two witnesses who can no longer testify to its authenticity," Livingstone finished for him. He was silent for a while, digesting the full implications. "A perfect motive for murder, I'd say."

"Right!" Taggart nodded emphatically. "The last time I smelt anything as fishy as this was on a trawler."

"You doubt the validity of this will?" Pearson asked. He sounded personally affronted. "I can assure you that Mr Mulholland's signature appears perfectly genuine to me."

Taggart smiled cynically. "That's what they said about the Hitler Diaries. I say we get a handwriting expert to go over these papers on the almost-certain assumption that all these signatures are forgeries."

"And check Mulholland's house for a typewriter," Livingstone added. "To my knowledge, we never saw one."

Taggart acknowledged this contribution with a faint nod. He was deep in thought. A minor brainwave finally struck him. "Maxwell," he blurted out suddenly.

Livingstone looked a little puzzled. The significance of the name had escaped him.

Taggart explained. "Maxwell . . . offices . . . typewriters. And Kirsty King worked for him."

"As a typist, amongst other things," Livingstone put in excitedly, finally following Taggart's thought patterns.

"Amongst other things is right." Taggart gave a knowing nod. "A rather amazing little chain of coincidence, wouldn't you say?"

Doubt suddenly furrowed Livingstone's brow, as the chain broke down in his mind. "But Kirsty King was the first to die."

Taggart looked a bit peeved. "Yes, that bothers me as well," he admitted. "A partner in crime, perhaps? A partner who decided they didn't want to split two ways after all?"

Livingstone nodded. "Yes, a definite possibility." He picked up the will again and glanced through it. "There's one more strange coincidence here . . . although it doesn't seem to fit with the others."

"Oh?" Taggart frowned, annoyed at the suggestion he should have missed something.

"This sole beneficiary," Livingstone went on. "This Dorothy Milner."

"What about her?"

"Remember Keith Brennan's alibi? For the Firhill murder? Well Dorothy Milner is the name of the woman in the dry cleaning shop."

Taggart looked down at Pearson's desk, imagining an almost-finished jigsaw puzzle into which Livingstone had just tossed a rogue piece. When he looked up again, his face was baffled. His eyes met Livingstone's who merely shrugged helplessly. He was unable to make any sense of it either.

Pearson merely regarded them both in total bewilderment, half convinced that two escaped lunatics had wandered into his office. The other half of his thoughts was a nasty, sneaking little feeling that something was about to screw up his nice, tidy paperwork.

Chapter Nineteen

DOROTHY MILNER turned over the 'Closed' sign on the door and returned to the counter, where Taggart and Livingstone waited for her. She looked a little shaken, Taggart thought. Why, he wasn't sure. Genuine surprise at her sudden good fortune? Alarm that two senior policemen should have brought the news? Or was she just a good actress?

"Why?" Taggart demanded, brusquely. He didn't feel like wasting time.

Dorothy paused before answering. Collecting herself? Or going over her story? Taggart seethed with irritation. He had never wished more that he see inside someone's head, read their thoughts.

"It was a long time ago," Dorothy started, in a hesitant voice. "Thirteen years, to be exact. It was just one of those silly things . . . a young girl's crush on a middle-aged man. I always thought it was just a bit on the side for him . . . but now, I'm not sure."

"How did you meet?" Livingstone asked.

Dorothy smiled distantly, as though recalling a fond memory. "At a bus stop, in the rain. I was coming home from school. Frank stopped and offered me a lift. We went for a coffee. I liked him. I could talk to him in a way I never talked to my father. There was nothing sexual in it at first . . . that came later."

"How old were you?" Taggart demanded.

"Seventeen. It was my last year."

"And how long did it last?"

"About a year. Cathy, his wife, never knew about it."

"Who broke it off?" Livingstone wanted to know.

Dorothy waved her hands vaguely. "It just finished . . . after the baby."

"Baby?" Taggart jumped on the word. "You had a baby by Frank Mulholland?"

Dorothy nodded. "I put it up for adoption. It seemed the best thing at the time. It was a little boy. I don't know what happened to him."

"So Mulholland stopped the affair when you became

131

pregnant?" Taggart prompted.

Dorothy shook her head. "No — it wasn't like that at all. We just . . . stopped seeing each other. Things ran their course, and then they were over. There was no bitterness, on either side. We stayed friends over the years . . . he'd still come into the shop, say hello . . . but that was it. I just never dreamed he'd thought about me all these years."

"Maybe he didn't, Miss Milner," Taggart said flatly.

Dorothy looked at him blankly. If she drew any inference from the words, she didn't let it show.

"Do the names Kirsty King and John Samson mean anything to you?" Taggart said suddenly, watching her face like a hawk. There was only a temporary frown of concentration before she answered.

"Well . . . yes. John Samson was Frank's son-in-law, and Kirsty King was that girl who died in the fire. Why do you ask?"

"The two witnesses to the will which makes you beneficiary. Both dead. I trust you'll be able to give us an account of your movements at the time of both deaths."

"Well, yes . . . I should think so." Dorothy looked puzzled. "Though I can't see what relevance . . ."

"It might have a great deal of relevance, Miss Milner," Taggart cut in. "We shall have to see, shan't we?"

Again, Dorothy betrayed no understanding that she was in any way under suspicion. Certainly there was no fear of discovery, Taggart decided. He had a strong feeling that her story would check right down to the very last detail. As, no doubt, it was intended to.

"There is just one last thing," Livingstone announced suddenly. Both Dorothy and Taggart looked at him in surprise. "You do realise that despite the will, Mr Mulholland's daughter is legally entitled to half of the moveable estate."

"You mean Eleanor Samson?" Dorothy asked. She sounded extremely surprised.

"You didn't realise that, then?" Livingstone said.

"A little legal nicety you didn't take into account?" Taggart added, building on his colleague's unexpected attack.

Dorothy looked at them both in confusion. "I'm not quite sure what you are both talking about. But Eleanor can't be entitled to any of Frank's estate, surely?"

"Oh . . . and why should that be?" Livingstone asked. He glanced awkwardly aside at Taggart, aware that matters seemed to be heading for an unexpected turn.

When it came, it was a bombshell.

"Because Eleanor Samson is not Frank's daughter," Dorothy announced, as though surprised neither detective was aware of the fact.

A policewoman ushered Eleanor into Taggart's office. Taggart rose to meet her, his face serious, but comforting. "Thank you for coming, Mrs Samson."

"I'm not sure if I need Mr Donaldson," Eleanor said, uncertainly. She looked at Taggart and Livingstone in turn.

"That won't be necessary, believe me," Taggart assured her. "This meeting is not an interrogation or an interview in any way." He gestured to the chair. "Please sit down and relax, Mrs Samson. And please accept my condolences for the loss of your father."

"Thank you." Eleanor seemed to accept Taggart's efforts at friendliness at face value. She sat down and composed herself.

"It's about your father's will, Mrs Samson," Livingstone said.

Eleanor's face clouded over with anger at the very mention of the will.

"I assume you have been informed of its rather . . . unusual contents?" Taggart said, even though Eleanor's expression had pre-empted the question.

"I wanted to see this spurious will," Eleanor said, in a coldly furious tone.

"You think it *is* spurious?"

"It has to be," Eleanor retorted, without the slightest trace of doubt.

"Then you have never heard of this woman, Dorothy Milner, before today?" Livingstone asked.

"Never, who is she? What possible right can she have to my father's estate?"

Eleanor was getting worked up into a bit of a state. Taggart tried to calm her down. "Before we come to that, let me say that I share your opinion that this will is a forgery." He paused, letting this degree of comfort sink in before moving on to more unpleasant topics. "It is also now my opinion that we have a clear motive for the murders of Kirsty King, your husband and your father."

Taggart had expected this revelation to come as a shock. He had not expected to see Eleanor Samson as near to complete breakdown. She flinched as though she had been struck violently. Her chest heaved as she fought to control her breathing. From somewhere deep in her stomach, she dredged up enough strength to croak out the single word. "John?"

"He was murdered, Mrs Samson," Taggart said gently. "As I believe your father was murdered."

Eleanor took a deep breath, fighting for control. Taggart waited, watching her, acutely aware of how sadly he had misjudged a brave woman.

"But the inquest verdict?" Eleanor whispered, finally.

"They were wrong. As we were wrong." Taggart looked pointedly at Livingstone as he spoke. Livingstone shifted uncomfortably in his seat, coughed nervously and looked away. As Taggart turned his attention back to Eleanor, he heard the faint sound of a chair scraping against the floor and Livingstone's footsteps towards the door. He was glad when the young man left the room.

"Please explain to me," Eleanor pleaded.

"Yes, of course." Taggart smiled gently, reassuringly. He took a breath. "Kirsty King and your husband witnessed this will . . . which I'm convinced will turn out to be a forgery. I think they were both murdered so that they could never give evidence should you or Graeme decide to contest it."

"And this woman . . . where does she come in?"

"Ah." Taggart felt a slight embarrassment. "Now I'm afraid we come to some rather delicate, personal matters. I'm sorry."

"It's all right. Please go on," Eleanor said, helping him in turn.

"Dorothy Milner claims that she had an affair with your father thirteen years ago, and that she had a son by him. Is that possible?"

Eleanor managed a hollow laugh. "You didn't know him. Yes, it's more than possible. He had affairs with several young girls."

Now came the really tricky bit, which Taggart was quietly dreading. "There is something else, Mrs Samson. I must warn you, it is of a highly personal nature and may come as a terrible shock to you."

Eleanor smiled mirthlessly. "*Another* shock? I'm not sure that word has much meaning to me at this moment."

"I'm afraid this will," Taggart said seriously. "Please try to prepare yourself."

Eleanor stared at him closely, recognising the genuine concern on his face. She breathed deeply a few times, finally nodding her head. "I'm ready."

"Miss Milner maintains that your father confided a very personal secret in her all those years ago. That he was, in fact, not your real father at all. That your birth was the result of your mother's adultery with another, unnamed man."

Taggart fell silent, waiting for Eleanor to digest this information. He watched her face with compassion, ready to offer whatever comfort and sympathy he could when the storm broke.

It never did. Instead of the news finally breaking Eleanor, she seemed to take some strange comfort from it. It was as though a great weight had been lifted from her mind. Her face suddenly became calm, her eyes distantly thoughtful.

"He was always cold towards me," she murmured. "I never understood why. It makes sense, now."

"Miss Milner's claims may not be true," Taggart reminded her.

Eleanor shrugged, as though she didn't care either way. "Why should she make something like that up?"

"Perhaps to add credibility to the rest of her story. Who knows?"

"If it *is* true . . . how does this affect my position, legally?"

"You would have no claim on your father's estate, I'm afraid. There is a simple way to disprove it, of course."

"You mean a blood test?"

"Yes."

"Will that necessarily constitute legal proof?"

"No, not absolute proof," Taggart admitted. "But it would give you a strong case in a court of law."

Eleanor sighed, resignedly. "So it all has to be dragged out in the open, does it? More scandal for the papers. Eleanor Samson, the illegitimate opera singer."

"I hope it won't come to that," Taggart said, meaning it sincerely. "If we can crack this Milner woman, get her to retract her story and disprove the will, nobody need ever know. I have handwriting experts examining the signatures right now."

Eleanor looked at him with slight surprise. "You wouldn't

pursue the matter . . . from a legal standpoint?"

"Why should we? It's police policy not to get involved in domestic matters."

"Thank you," Eleanor said.

"Thank me? What for?"

"For not always being a policeman," Eleanor said.

Chapter Twenty

BRENNAN was drunk for the third day running. The third day of waiting for that fateful knock on the door, facing Taggart, knowing that Petrie had spilled the beans at last. It could only be a matter of time, Brennan was sure. Drinking didn't take away the dreadful sense of foreboding, but it helped cloud the clarity of his waking nightmares. Of bars, and steel doors, padlocks, and grim-faced wardens.

Lilly had, mistakenly, assumed he was still in a state of shock following Olive's death, and had been unusually sympathetic. Now, however, her limited patience was wearing thin.

She came in from doing the shopping chores, which Brennan normally undertook, in an irritable frame of mind, made immediately worse by the sight of his unshaven, bleary-eyed face and the half-finished bottle of whisky in his hand. "That stuff'll no bring her back, Keith Brennan — and it's high time you pulled yourself together."

"I'm not feeling well, Lilly," Brennan whined.

"All you're feeling is the bite of the barley," Lilly threw back at him, nodding at the whisky bottle. She snatched the bottle from his hand. "Now you just get back on your feet and pull your weight. I've had enough of doing your errands for you."

"Did you get my suits from the cleaners?" Brennan asked, reminded that they were overdue.

"I'm not your packhorse. I just looked in the shop. That was enough for me. You'll not catch me talking to the likes of her. Flighty little piece. I can see now why you go round there so often."

"I don't know what you're talking about." Brennan was sober enough to know Lilly was getting at something, but too befuddled to understand.

"She was old man Mulholland's littly fancy piece ... that's what I'm talking about. He's left her his fortune. Fine wages for laying on your back." Lilly looked at her husband's blank and bloodshot eyes and tired of trying to talk sensibly to him. She fished the evening paper from her bag and tossed it at him. "Here — read it for yourself. It's all in there. And they've charged that little swine who killed Olive at last. I hope they give him life."

Brennan jerked into sudden awareness. "They've charged him?"

"Aye, committed for trial, it says."

"Anything else? Like him having an accomplice or something?"

"An accomplice? What are you blethering about?" Lilly gave up in disgust and stalked off.

Brennan snatched up the paper and began to scan the headlines frantically. Jimmy Petrie rated only a small paragraph at the bottom of the front page. The item was brief. Just as Lilly had said, it reported only that the youth had been charged with murder and committed for prosecution.

The headline story caught Brennan's attention.

ELEANOR SAMSON'S FATHER FOUND DEAD
it screamed. Underneath the headline were captioned pictures of Kirsty King, John Samson, Frank Mulholland and Dorothy Milner. Brennan began to read the accompanying story carefully. The more he read, the more something niggled in the back of his mind. His eyes kept coming back to Mulholland's picture, as if it were some sort of clue. Whatever it was, it refused to surface. Yet it was important, Brennan knew. Something which might have a vital bearing on his predicament.

McVitie had nominated his office for the meeting on the pretext that it was bigger than Taggart's. Taggart knew this for the lame excuse it was. His superior was merely smarting from having been pushed out of things and wanted to get back in. Still, he had little choice but to go along with it, so McVitie's office it was.

Taggart and Livingstone stood, bending over McVitie's desk to study the post-mortem report which Dr Andrews had laid out for inspection. Perhaps because of McVitie's presence, Andrews was at his most pompous. "Massive Myocardial Infraction. Destruction of an area of heart muscle caused by the occlusion of a coronary artery."

"And in English?" Taggart asked, sarcastically.

"He had a heart attack," Livingstone put in brightly.

Taggart glanced sideways, lip curling. "Thank you, Doctor Frankenstein." He turned back to Andrews. "What does that mean, exactly?"

"It means goodbye to your murder theory, Jim," McVitie said.

Taggart was sure there was a gloating tone in his superior's voice, but he forced himself to ignore it. "What about the third degree burning down his side?' he asked Andrews. "He must have been lying in front of that electric fire for hours . . ."

"Secondary . . . and irrelevant, Jim," Andrews said, almost apologetically. "Coronary occlusion, plain and simple. I did every possible test. There's no room for doubt."

"Damn." Taggart gave vent to his feelings of frustration by slamming his bunched fist down on McVitie's desk.

"Easy, Jim. Mulholland had a history of cardiac trouble. We knew that," McVitie reminded him.

"Yes," Taggart sighed deeply. "We didn't know he owned a bloody typewriter though, did we?"

It was an afternoon when everything possible was going wrong. Theories were falling apart, apparent clues were evaporating into thin air, and coincidences were being neatly explained. Taggart was at boiling point, and had been ever since the typewriter had been discovered locked in Mulholland's desk, with only his fingerprints on it.

"And the will is genuine," McVitie reminded Taggart, rubbing salt in raw wounds.

"The *signatures* appear genuine," Taggart corrected him. It was a subtle difference, but an important one, he felt. "Somebody could have typed the will on Mulholland's typewriter, wearing gloves, and got the signatures afterwards. How many people sign things without reading them properly?"

"Hard-headed businessmen like Mulholland and Samson?" McVitie was openly sceptical, even mocking.

"So it was the old paper underneath trick," Taggart suggested, clutching at straws. "Besides . . . why should a hard-headed businessman sign a paper putting a small financial empire into the hands of a totally inexperienced young woman?"

"That's a good point," Livingstone said, partly because he agreed and partly because he felt sorry for Taggart.

Taggart snapped at the proffered olive branch. "It's a *bloody* good point." He paused for a moment, considering possible moves. When he had decided, he addressed McVitie. "I want to put a 24-hour watch on this Milner woman. If she didn't kill Kirsty King and John Samson, then somebody did it for her."

"And Mulholland's death? What about that?"

Taggart had to shrug helplessly. There, he was baffled. "It's not often we get a perfect motive without a murder, I admit."

"Two days, Jim . . . no more," McVitie said. "We can't spare the manpower."

"All right." Taggart accepted the short period of grace hopefully. They might just turn something up in 48 hours.

"Well . . . if you won't be needing me any more . . ." Andrews murmured.

Taggart grabbed at his sleeve in desperation. "There must be ways of inducing a heart attack. Shock?"

Andrews was sympathetic, but unable to offer Taggart the straw he was clutching for. "A hard word to define in law, Jim . . . and almost impossible to prove. Sorry."

"Yeah." Taggart let him go, reluctantly.

Brennan tossed fretfully in his bed, unable to sleep yet again but almost relieved that he couldn't. With sleep came the nightmares — Olive's bloody head, the sickening sound of a hammer-head crunching bone. And the screams . . . the horrible, stomach-churning screams.

He sat up suddenly, sweating and shivering at the same time. Had he been dreaming after all? The tiny flicker of hope died as soon as it was born in his whisky-sodden mind. No, it was all real. Petrie, the photographs, the plan . . .Olive's brutal murder. Even more terrifying than the reality was the knowledge that he would have to live with it for the rest of his life. It would be the sword of Damocles, poised over his head . . . but with a two-edged blade. On the one hand would always be the fear that Petrie would talk, that he would be caught and punished. On the other hand he was living with the terrible guilt if he wasn't.

The guilt. Somehow Brennan feared that worst. He wasn't sure he could cope with it. If only he were a Catholic — then at least he could make confession, protected by the Papal laws. That, above all, was what Brennan craved at that moment. A confessor — someone who could expiate his guilt by sharing it, without betraying him.

For no apparent reason, the newspaper picture of Mulholland

popped into his mind accompanied by an image of the dry-cleaning shop, with Dorothy behind the counter.

The image expanded, assuming a definite place and time. The day of the murder ... the time of fixing his alibi. Himself, Dorothy and Mulholland all in the shop together. Brennan saw a close-up of Mulholland's mouth as he spelled out the letters of his name. M-U-L-L . . .

Suddenly, Brennan knew that niggling, important thing which had eluded him earlier that evening.

As he suddenly knew who his confessor was to be. And why.

Chapter Twenty-one

BRENNAN looked ghastly. Wild-eyed, with two days of stubble and uncombed hair. Dorothy Milner hardly recognised him. For a moment, she thought a dangerous drunk had staggered off the streets into the shop and was about to attack her. She was about to run to the rear of the shop and lock herself in when she realised who it was.

"Hello," she said, nervously.

Brennan said nothing. He just stood there, staring at her with a vacant, half-crazy look on his face.

"Are you all right?" Dorothy asked. She wondered if he was ill, or had been in a traffic accident. There was no answer. Just the strange, penetrating stare. "Have you come for your suits?" Dorothy asked, after a while.

Brennan shook his head slowly from side to side. He backed slowly to the shop door and slid the catch across, locking it. Turning the 'Closed' sign round, he confronted Dorothy once more, finally speaking. "There was a murder . . . in my pub."

Dorothy was now almost convinced that there was something seriously wrong with him. "Yes, I heard about it," she said, humouring him. She wondered whether to make a dash for the telephone, to call the police.

"A murder," Brennan repeated, as though the word should hold some special significance for her.

"Yes, I heard you. What are you trying to say?" Dorothy was feeling edgy now, sensing a threat which had nothing to do with physical violence.

"I thought you'd be interested," Brennan said. "Something we had in common. Like being in the same business."

Dorothy's eyes narrowed. "What do you want?"

"Just to talk. I hear you've inherited a lot of money."

Dorothy was glad for the change of subject. "Yes. A man I was once very close to," she said, with forced enthusiasm.

"Mullholland. M-U-L-L-"

The sensed threat was assuming definite shape now. Dorothy felt a cold prickle down her back. She decided to try and bluff it out. "I have no idea what you're talking about."

"I was here . . . in the shop . . . that day. When Mulholland had to spell his name out for you. I thought it was funny at the time . . . you pretended to know him . . . *but he didn't know you.*"

The bluff had failed, Dorothy realised with resignation. Brennan *knew*. She glared at him with undisguised hate. "What do you want? Money? Blackmail, is that it?"

Brennan was confused by her antagonism. He had expected sympathy, understanding, the shared bond of two people in the same terrible trouble. He felt rejected, abandoned. He stared at her dumbly for several moments.

Wrongly, Dorothy took his silence to be an affirmation of her suspicions. "Come back tomorrow," she hissed at him. "I'll see what I can do. Now just get out of here."

Brennan backed away under the sheer intensity of her loathing. Turning, he stumbled to the door, unlocked it and fled into the street outside.

Dorothy stood rigidly for a while, her attractive face contorted into a frightened and angry mask. Finally, she moved to the telephone and dialled a local number. "It's Dorothy. Somebody knows. We'll either have to pay him off . . . or kill him."

From his vantage point across the street, Livingstone had observed the entire scene through a pair of binoculars. He felt a sense of elation. It seemed that Taggart's hunch was paying off sooner than expected.

Taggart was equally pleased with the news, but he was wary of any false leads. "You're sure Brennan didn't go into the shop on a normal errand?"

Livingstone shook his head. "He went in empty-handed and came out the same way. He seemed very agitated. Dorothy Milner made a single telephone call, then locked up the shop for the day and left immediately afterwards. It's a busy shopping day. There was something up, I'm sure of it."

"Did you follow her?"

"As far as I could. She got on a bus. I didn't want her to recognise me — put her on the alert."

Taggart nodded thoughtfully. "Probably the best decision. Let's put Brennan under surveillance as well and wait for their next little get-together. Hopefully, they'll lead us right to the heart of this damned business." He broke off to give vent to a thoughtful little chuckle. "Well, who'd have thought it would turn out to be Keith Brennan who's involved with our little Miss Clean-Easy?"

"You think *he* killed Kirsty King and Samson?" Livingstone asked.

"If he did, she must have put him up to it. Turned his head, as they say. After Lilly, I suppose it's almost understandable."

"But then where does Olive MacQueen's murder fit into all this?"

Taggart shook his head in total bewilderment. "That's the part I can't figure out," he admitted.

Chapter Twenty-two

LIVINGSTONE announced, "Here he comes."

Taggart took the binoculars from Livingstone's fingers, focused them on the figure of Brennan, walking through the precinct towards the dry-cleaning shop. He checked his watch with a quick downward glance. "Two minutes after opening time. Something must be urgent."

"It's not dry-cleaning, that's for sure," Livingstone said. He didn't need the binoculars to see that Brennan was once more empty-handed. The second time in two days.

"Funny," Taggart observed. "I wouldn't have thought Keith had the guts to commit murder."

"Or the brains."

Taggart looked at his colleague with recent, but growing respect. "You've figured that one out, then?"

"That our killer is clever?" Livingstone smiled. "Oh yes. If they ever awarded IQ points for murder, our man would have to be on the 97th percentile . . . at least."

"So you think Keith . . ."

"Is a pawn, who fits somewhere into the game."

"Or a red herring?" Taggart suggested. He clapped Livingstone on the shoulder. "Let's find out, shall we?"

It was a rare moment of camaraderie between the two men. Surprisingly, Livingstone realised he enjoyed it. He followed Taggart's lead, striding across the traffic-free road towards the dry-cleaning shop.

Brennan entered the shop. Dorothy had seen him coming, and was ready for him. Under the counter, her hands were already clasped around a loosely-wrapped paper parcel. With a furtive glance outside, she lifted the parcel on to the counter top as Brennan approached.

"There's twenty thousand in there. It's the only payment you'll get. Just take it and go."

Dorothy thrust the parcel forward. More out of surprise than anything else, Brennan picked it up. Absently, he picked at the brown wrapping paper, opening it just enough to see the bundles of banknotes inside. He stared at Dorothy blankly.

"Go," she hissed again, with urgency in her voice.

Brennan just stood there, his mouth opening like a suffocating fish.

Over his shoulder, Dorothy saw Taggart and Livingstone stepping up on to the pavement, heading directly for the shop front. Panicking, she reached forwards and snatched the parcel back out of Brennan's hands, whisking it away out of sight and under the counter again. She just had time to snap out a few words before Taggart pushed open the door. "For God's sake just act normal."

Brennan saw the panic in her eyes and whirled round at the sound of the door opening. The first thing Taggart and Livingstone saw was his face, wide-eyed and staring, like a little boy caught with his hand in the biscuit jar.

"Guilty as Hell," Taggart thought. He adopted a knowing smile for Brennan's benefit. "Well, well, Keith. You're a frequent visitor here lately. Got a lot of dirty laundry, have we?"

Brennan raised a sickly smile. "Hello, Mr Taggart."

Dorothy had slipped neatly into her role as the efficient shopkeeper. She smiled sweetly at Livingstone. "Good morning. And how can I help you this morning? I'll just finish serving this customer and I'll be right with you."

She turned back to Brennan. "Let's see . . . two suits, wasn't it? I'll look them out for you."

Dorothy retreated into the rear of the shop, searching the racks for Brennan's two suits. Finding them, she carried them to the counter. One of the suits had a piece of paper pinned to it. A reminder. Dorothy read it, responding exactly as she would under normal circumstances. "Oh yes . . . you left something in one of the pockets. I'll get it for you." She moved along the counter to a filing tray, picking out a brown envelope.

Brennan felt the world collapsing on top of him. Over-reacting, he clawed out for the envelope with quivering fingers.

Taggart's hand intercepted the envelope, snatching it from Dorothy's fingers. He prised open the top flap, fishing inside for the contents. "Been taking some more photographs, Keith? I'd like to see them, if you don't mind."

Brennan's shoulders almost slumped as Taggart pulled out two photographs and laid them on the counter.

"Well, well, Peter," Taggart muttered. It would seem our Keith here has been keeping some bad company."

Livingstone looked down at the two prints. One showed Petrie in the act of stabbing the Telecom engineer. The other one was of him running away from the telephone box.

Taggart's hand was like a vice on Brennan's shoulder. "Looks like we've got some talking to do," he said thickly.

The talking hadn't taken long. Brennan had needed a confessor, and he'd found two extremely willing ones in Taggart and Livingstone. Now that he had poured out his guilt, he felt calmer, more or less resigned to his fate.

"What'll happen to me?"

"You'll be charged with conspiracy to pervert the course of justice, and accessory to murder," Taggart said flatly. "If there's any justice at all, you'll get a longer stretch than Petrie does. I hope they put you and the kid in the same place."

Brennan shuddered at the thought. "But the information I gave you . . . about Mulholland and that Milner woman . . . you'll make sure that's taken into consideration?"

"I'll see what I can do," Taggart promised him. He looked up at the constable on door duty and signalled with his eyes. He looked across at Livingstone with a wry smile as Brennan was taken away to the cells.

"Well, Peter. We were watching two different football matches all the time. They got their balls crossed."

Livingstone's face was grim. He was still appalled by Brennan's revelations. "Five thousand pounds to bash someone's skull in with a hammer," he muttered, as though he still couldn't quite believe it.

Taggart could, and did, believe it — quite easily. "You tell me what the *union* rate is," he said, cynically. "It probably seemed like a small fortune to someone like Jimmy Petrie."

Livingstone conceded the point with a faint nod. "So — we now know that Dorothy Milner's story is a fabrication," he said, getting back to the business in hand.

"All we have to do is prove it . . . and find out who put her up to it."

"Any ideas?" Livingstone should have known better than to

expect a straight answer.

"Have you?" Taggart merely countered. They were both silent for some time, thinking deeply.

"There is one little thing which keeps tickling away in the back of my mind," Livingstone said uncertainly, at long last.

Taggart snapped at it. He was ready to take anything, however vague or tenuous. "What? Think!"

Livingstone frowned, concentrating his thoughts. "The day I first interviewed Dorothy Milner . . . when I was checking Keith's alibi. A woman started to come into the shop . . . and it seemed as though Dorothy Milner panicked for a moment. She slammed and locked the door in her face. It was almost as though she didn't want me to meet her."

Taggart was hooked. "Now *this* could be interesting," he mused. "Can you remember any details about this woman? Think of any time or place you might have seen her before? Any connection with Samson or Mulholland?"

Livingstone was struggling to remember. There *was* something . . . one tiny detail which hadn't seemed particularly important at the time. It came, suddenly, in one of those strange little quirks of memory. "She'd just had a perm," Livingstone blurted out. "That's it . . . her hair had that fresh, just too perfect to be true look . . . as though she had just that moment walked out of a hairdressing salon."

It didn't seem like much, but it was all they had. Taggart considered carefully for a while. "There's a salon in the precinct . . . about six or seven doors down from the dry-cleaning shop," he remembered. "It might be worth checking out their appointments book for that day."

"Could be a long shot . . . and a lot of footwork," Livingstone pointed out. "Can we spare the manpower?"

"Oh, I think so." Taggart was grinning all over his face.

Livingstone knew the look . . . and what it meant. His face fell. "You want *me* to do it?"

Taggart nodded, gleefully. "It's called delegation, Peter."

"I'll get straight on to it," Livingstone muttered resentfully. "And what will you be doing?"

"Me? I'm going to Mulholland's funeral," Taggart announced.

Chapter Twenty-three

THE HAIRDRESSER was male, obviously gay, and obviously much taken with tall young policemen. Livingstone squirmed uncomfortably as the crimper camped it up outrageously, going out of his way to be helpful.

"Now dear . . . you say she had brownish hair, medium length with no highlights, and she'd had a fresh perm?"

"That's it," Livingstone agreed with a nod. They had arrived at the brief description by a process of elimination.

"No problem, dear. I'll get you the names and addresses of all the likely candidates."

Livingstone was surprised — and impressed. "You've got addresses?"

"Oh yes, dearie. On a card index file. All perm customers are on file . . . so we can order up the correct colours and perm solutions for the next appointment."

It was an unexpectedly lucky break. Livingstone waited impatiently as the hairdresser flipped through the files. He finally pulled out six cards. "Here you are. It could be any one of these six. I'd love to help you more, dear, but you didn't give me much to go on."

"That's just fine," Livingstone assured him. He copied down the six names and addresses quickly and made a discreet exit.

Eleanor answered the door to Taggart's knock. She was neatly dressed in a fetching black two-piece which managed to look sober yet elegant at the same time.

"Do you want to come in?"

Taggart nodded through the open doorway behind her. "Is there anyone else in the house?"

"Yes. Graeme and Don. They're still getting dressed."

"I'd like a private talk, Mrs Samson. Private . . . and personal."

"We'll walk in the garden," Eleanor said. She stepped out, pulling the door to behind her.

"I'd like you to know that no charges will be brought against you," Taggart told her, breaking the good news first. "Lack of evidence."

"That sounds like a face-saving decision," Eleanor murmured.

Taggart was surprised at the apparent calmness with which she took the announcement. "I thought you'd feel relieved."

Eleanor shrugged. "I don't feel anything. Except that this business will always be hanging over me now. Murder not proven. There will always be people who think I did it. Audiences will come to the opera for all the wrong reasons."

"Oh, I doubt that." Taggart tried to sound convincing, and failed.

Eleanor smiled at him. "Why have you tried to help me?"

Taggart felt slightly embarrassed. "Let's just say I'm an admirer."

There was a faint twinkle in Eleanor's eye. "My admirers don't fall asleep while I'm performing."

"Ah!" Taggart looked suitably sheepish. He strolled a few more paces before speaking again. "We know that Dorothy Milner is lying, now. She never knew your father. Someone concocted this whole story and got her in to play a role. That someone knew your father very well."

Eleanor wasn't really listening. "My father," she murmured, distantly. "Strange how that word has such a hollow ring to it now."

It brought Taggart to the main — and unpleasant — reason for his visit. "We have the results of the blood test," he announced, gently. "I thought I'd be the one to break it to you."

"So it's true?"

Taggart nodded sadly. "Frank Mulholland's blood group was AA. Yours is O. That makes it impossible . . ."

Eleanor cut him short. "I think I knew, from the very first moment. Perhaps I always knew, even as a little girl." She broke off, choking back a sob. "I wonder who my father really was?"

Taggart was strangely moved. He felt that he wanted to put his arms around her, hold her tight, feel her tears against his cheek. "I wish I could tell you," he said sadly, lamely.

Eleanor pulled herself up with an effort. She seemed to notice that Taggart was wearing a black suit and tie for the first time. "You're coming to the funeral?" She sounded surprised.

Taggart nodded. "It's normal police procedure," he said, neglecting to add that it was to view the mourners as potential murder suspects.

"Perhaps you'd like to ride in the car with me?" Eleanor suggested.

Taggart accepted graciously. "Yes, thank you."

They walked slowly back towards the house.

Livingstone parked outside a neat little detached bungalow and checked the address against his list. Four names were already crossed off. Sighing, he climbed out of the car to go through the whole procedure one more time. He walked up the short drive and rang the bell. A man answered.

Livingstone showed his ID card. "Sorry to bother you. Is Mrs Marr at home?"

The man grinned. "What's she done this time? Parked on another double yellow line?"

"Nothing like that," Livingstone assured him. "I just need to talk to her, as a possible witness."

"Afraid she's at work at the moment. You could go and see her at the surgery, if it's that important."

"Surgery?" Livingstone felt his stomach jolt as he seized on the word.

"Yes — Doctor MacNaughton's surgery — my wife is the receptionist there."

Livingstone had already turned his back and was racing for the car. It all made sense, suddenly. The last piece had fallen into the jigsaw, completing the picture. Livingstone could only hope that he would be in time.

He jumped into his car, fired it into life and pulled away with a squeal of tyres, heading for the crematorium.

The mourners filed into the small chapel. Taggart walked behind Eleanor, letting her go ahead as they went inside. As she carried on to join close relatives in the front row, Taggart seated himself at the very back, with a good view of everyone present.

Dorothy Milner came in alone, looking out of place in black. She walked down the aisle slowly, as heads turned towards her. For a while, she was the focal point of attention. The Scarlet Woman — Mulholland's mistress — heiress to his millions.

Dorothy ignored the glances and the hushed whispers. She looked aside only once, at Ted Maxwell, exchanging a brief and discreet nod of recognition. She sat down alone, apart from the other mourners.

Taggart had taken it all in. He had made a mental note of all those people who had paid particular attention to her . . . and those who had not. Behind him, an attendant started to close the door. Piped organ music started up. The vicar stepped up to the podium to begin reading the service. Taggart wondered how Livingstone was getting on.

Livingstone screamed into the crematorium car park and jumped out of his car without switching off the engine. He looked at the front of the chapel, noting the locked doors and the faint sound of organ music. Stirrings of panic seized him. There wasn't much time left.

He turned his gaze around the car park, identifying MacNaughton's vehicle by the 'Doctor On Call' sticker in the windscreen. He moved to it quickly, peering in through the windows. MacNaughton's bag and briefcase lay on the back seat. Livingstone ran round the car, trying all the doors. They were locked.

He seethed with frustration. So close . . . so little time . . . and professional ethics to contend with. Livingstone tossed this last consideration from his mind with a mental gesture of bravado. He'd had no time to check his theories. All he had was an assumption . . . his "copper's nose" as Taggart called it. Ah well! He might as well hang for a sheep as a lamb. Livingstone scoured the crematorium grounds for a suitable blunt instrument.

Against a side wall of the chapel, he found a small pile of bricks left over from an extension building project. He picked one up and carried it to MacNaughton's car. Taking a quick glance over his shoulder and mouthing a silent prayer that he was right, Livingstone smashed in the rear side window. Opening the door, he pulled out MacNaughton's black bag and began to rummage through its contents.

The assortment of drugs and medical instruments confused him. He wasn't even sure what he was looking for. He tried a process of elimination, putting aside things which seemed normal or which he recognised from his crash course in forensic medicine at the police training academy.

Eventually, he was left with one small phial containing white powder, bearing a long and complicated label which meant nothing to him. He carried it across to his own car and snapped on the police radio.

"This is Livingstone to Control. I have to get a very urgent message to Doctor Andrews. Tell him I need some information about a drug called Suxamethonium Bromide. I want to know this: What does it do? Would a GP normally carry it? And could the burning in Mulholland's side have disguised the track of a hypodermic needle? And tell him I need all this in the next few minutes."

Livingstone put down the radio, slipped the phial into his pocket and walked back to MacNaughton's car. He reached in for the briefcase and opened it, spreading its contents out on the back seat. There was a sheaf of Deeds of Covenant, relating to the Heathervale Hospice for the Terminally Ill. Flipping through them, Livingstone found that Kirsty King, John Samson and Frank Mulholland had all made donations. Their signatures were on the Deeds, and on Bankers' Orders attached.

Livingstone straightened up, grinning to himself. So Taggart *had* been right after all. The old paper underneath trick. So *that* was how MacNaughton had obtained flawless signatures.

The smile faded as he remembered the urgency of the situation. He ran back to his car and snatched up the radio. "Any news from Dr Andrews yet?"

There was a crackle of static and a female voice.

"I think he has something for you. Hold on ... I'm patching you through now."

Livingstone waited, tapping his foot impatiently until Andrews came on the line. He sounded more than usually tetchy. "What's this all about, young man? Do you think I'm at your personal beck and call twenty-four hours a day?"

Livingstone was terse. "Just give me the answers, Doc. This is vital."

"Very well." MacNaughton paused, consulting his text-book in front of him. "Suxamethonium Bromide is used as a special anaesthetic during surgery. It acts by relaxing the muscles for particularly delicate operations. Too much of it will cause death by failure of the chest muscles to maintain breathing. It is virtually undetectable, breaking down into succinic acid and choline, both of which are normally present in tissue. I believe it figured in a sensational murder case in America some twenty years ago. Now that I know what I'm looking for, I can find a trace ... but we'll prove nothing without the body."

"Thanks Doc." Livingstone dropped the radio mike on to the car seat and sprinted for the back entrance of the crematorium.

The short service was completed. The music ceased. With a faint whine, the conveyor belt started up, carrying Mulholland's flower-bedecked coffin through the curtains between the chapel and the incinerator room. Taggart watched it disappear and rose from his seat quickly whilst the other mourners observed a two-minute silence.

Behind the curtain, two operators slid Mulholland's coffin from the end of the conveyor belt on to a wheeled trolley. They trundled it away through a set of swing doors towards the incinerator room. Moments later, the whine of machinery started up, winding up the heavy steel doors of the furnace.

Livingstone reached the back door, wrestling with the knob. It was locked. Frantically, he pounded on the door with his clenched fists, shouting, "Police. Urgent. Open up at once."

It seemed ages before a voice answered. "Hold on. What do you want?"

Livingstone repeated his message. "This is the police. Open up at once, this is urgent."

There was the sound of a bolt being drawn back and the door opened. "Urgent, is it? Matter of life and death, eh?"

Livingstone didn't have time to appreciate the black joke, or to show his ID. He pushed rudely past the crematorium worker, rushing through the intervening doors into the incinerator room. He was just in time to see the furnace door close tight, and one of the workers press the ignition button. The furnace snapped into life and with a dull whoosh and a roar of flames.

"Get that body out of there," Livingstone yelled. "Switch off the gas — now!"

The operator looked at him as though he was mad. "You're kidding. It's a raging inferno in there. Besides — it's an automatic system. You can't stop it."

Livingstone cursed out loud. He slammed his clenched fists against his sides in impotent fury.

"Peter . . . over here." Taggart's voice drew his attention, summoning him towards a small ante-room.

Livingstone walked in. Taggart stood there, a huge grin on his face. He was leaning on a coffin. "I hope you're not late for your own."

Livingstone did a double-take for a moment, not quite understanding. Finally he nodded at the coffin. "Mulholland?" he said, hardly daring to believe it.

Taggart nodded. "Aye. They had a backlog. Well?"

"MacNaughton," Livingstone said. "He used a drug called Suxamethonium Bromide."

"Aye, it had to be something," Taggart said, nodding sagely.

Livingstone regarded him in amazement. "You knew?"

"Pretty sure," Taggart said casually. "He was the only man in that congregation who didn't even glance at Miss Clean-Easy. And who better than a GP to stumble upon the little family skeleton which gave rise to the whole idea? An accidental comparison of Mulholland's and Eleanor's blood types? Perhaps old man Mulholland even confided the secret in him at some time. And who else could have intercepted the confirmation from the bank? MacNaughton always visited Mulholland early in the mornings. Plus the almost clinical precision of the murders. There were plenty of clues . . . what we needed was proof."

"Which is what I've got," Livingstone announced proudly, producing the phial of drug from his pocket.

"Good boy, Peter," Taggart said, as if he were a dog. "Well . . . shall we go and get him?"

MacNaughton was already at his car examining the damage as Taggart and Livingstone emerged into the car park. Seeing them, he drew their attention. "Look at this. Some blasted vandals have broken into my car."

"No vandal, Doctor MacNaughton," Livingstone said quietly. "It was me. I was looking for this." He pulled the phial from his pocket once more, displaying it.

MacNaughton's face froze, momentarily. Then he glanced up, saw the smoke pouring from the crematorium chimney and relaxed. He was safe. He smiled defiantly.

Taggart decided to wipe it from his face — permanently. "That's another body. We still have Mulholland. It'll take some time to complete the tests, of course, but I might as well caution

155

you now."

MacNaughton stared into Taggart's steely eyes, searching for a trace of bluff and finding none. He slumped against the side of his car, beaten and hopeless. "I thought I'd committed the perfect murder," he muttered.

"Oh, you had," Taggart assured him. "The trouble was — someone else's unfortunately got in the way."

From the corner of his eye, Livingstone saw Dorothy Milner emerge from the chapel, look across at them and stop dead in her tracks. He turned, poising himself to give chase as she made a panic decision and decided to make a run for it.

He wasn't quite quick enough. Dorothy made a break for her car and jumped in, locking the doors from inside. By the time Livingstone reached it, she already had the ignition key in the lock, and was turning it. He could only beat his hands futilely against the windows as Dorothy slammed the car into gear and took off down the crematorium drive like a bat out of hell.

Even though it seemed pointless, Livingstone broke into a run after the speeding car. His long legs flashed over the gravel drive with the grace and precision of a professional athlete. There was an almost magical quality about his movement. If a man *could* chase a car and catch it, it would be a man who ran like Livingstone.

Perhaps it was this unreality, this sense of inexorable pursuit, which made Dorothy panic. She was at the gates of the crematorium, with a good fifty yards on Livingstone and time to stop whilst the last two cars of another cortege came through.

She didn't even slow down. The front of her car smashed head-on into the side of a black Daimler, throwing her head-first against the windscreen. She was still dazed when Livingstone reached the car, wrenched open the burst front door and pulled her out bodily.

Dazed . . . but not completely out of fight. Feigning weakness, she slumped against him, looking for the right moment and the right position. It came as Livingstone shifted his legs apart to brace himself against her dead weight.

Dorothy brought her knee up savagely, with every ounce of strength she could muster. It connected low under his groin, swamping his body and brain in a searing wave of agony. He sank slowly towards the ground, his body contorted with pain.

Dorothy turned to run, only to find her path blocked by two of the drivers from the funeral cortege. Reading the situation accurately, they moved in to grab hold of her, restraining her as she kicked and screamed and spat until the last ounce of energy was drained from her body.

From a distance, Taggart watched as Livingstone dragged himself to his feet and hobbled painfully across to the quiescent Dorothy. Taggart winced, thinking about that knee in the groin.

He turned away, a faint, secretive grin breaking out on his face. It must have been a painful lesson for his young colleague. But it *was* a lesson, and Livingstone was learning.

One day — perhaps soon, Taggart thought — he was going to make a damned good copper.